Step into the new, strange world of the future and you will be both amazed and horrified. Join Mara as she is forced to set sail when her Scottish island disappears under the flood waters; Becca, who discovers the value of pets in the course of a history project; Jim, whose virtual reality travels lead him to the truth about his father; and Jack, who discovers to his horror that he has been cloned to provide body parts.

These ten mind-boggling stories have been summoned up by the imaginations of exciting authors like Jan Mark, Lesley Howarth and Julie Bertagna.

Also available by Tony Bradman,
and published by Corgi Books:

GOOD SPORTS! A BAG OF SPORTS STORIES
FANTASTIC SPACE STORIES
AMAZING ADVENTURE STORIES
INCREDIBLY CREEPY STORIES
SENSATIONAL CYBER STORIES
GRIPPING WAR STORIES

PHENOMENAL
FUTURE
STORIES

Collected by Tony Bradman

Illustrated by Peter Dennis

CORGI BOOKS

PHENOMENAL FUTURE STORIES
A CORGI BOOK : 0 552 54963 0

First publication in Great Britain

This edition produced for the Book People Ltd,
Hall Wood Avenue, Haydock, St Helens, WA11 9UL

PRINTING HISTORY
Corgi edition published 1999

Set in 12/14.5pt Bembo by
Phoenix Typesetting, Ilkley, West Yorkshire

Corgi Books are published by Transworld Publishers,
61–63 Uxbridge Road, Ealing, London W5 5SA,
a division of The Random House Group Ltd,
in Australia by Random House Australia (Pty) Ltd,
20 Alfred Street, Milsons Point, Sydney, NSW 2061, Australia,
in New Zealand by Random House New Zealand Ltd,
18 Poland Road, Glenfield, Auckland 10, New Zealand
and in South Africa by Random House (Pty) Ltd,
Endulini, 5a Jubilee Road, Parktown 2193, South Africa.

Printed and bound in Great Britain by
Cox & Wyman Ltd, Reading, Berkshire.

CONTENTS

AMPHIBIAN CITY
by Julie Bertagna

The island is gone.

A whole island swallowed in the night.

News came in the early hours on radio waves so fuzzed we could still pretend we'd misheard. No-one really believed it would come to this. We'd watched the seas eat away our shores, then reach hungrily up the hillsides towards the village, yet still we'd hoped against hope for a miracle that would gentle the seas.

But when daylight dawned the northern horizon lay empty except for the scattered fleet of boats heading south – refugees from the sunken island.

Now it's too late for miracles and we have to believe. The great flat island is gone. And any day now the rising sea will take us too.

★

'Go now, Mara,' says Tain. 'Go and find a new future.'

Gently, he pushes me towards the boat. Mum, Dad and the little ones are already launched but I wouldn't go till the last, still hoping a place might be found for Tain. I clutch at his sleeve as I did when I was little and tagged along with him as he stacked the peat and turned the cheeses. His wee helper, he called me.

But I can't help Tain now. There are to be no old ones on the refugee boats. All the old ones are to stay on the drowning island.

'The boats can't take us all. Tell me who to leave – the old folk or the children? The brown-eyed or the blue?' Alex, our skipper, challenges me. But he is shamefaced and desperate. The old folk stand by the harbour, dead-eyed and resigned.

The journey south will be treacherous. Maybe none of us will survive. And even if we reach the city port we don't know what we face there. Government broadcasts tell us to stay in our homes, that the city will not admit refugees. Outlaw radio reports on a barricaded city and boat villages which are becoming increasingly squalid. But if we stay in our homes we drown.

Unable to look at Tain, I take my seat in the boat. I know there is little chance of survival for an old man with a weak heart in wild seas or in a boat village. And to take him away from his beloved island, even now, would break his heart.

Tain waves goodbye and I know that the fear on his face is for me, for all of us. Not for himself, the abandoned one.

Two hundred years the world has had to stop the global warming that's melted the polar ice caps and raised the seas; two whole centuries to change our careless, selfish ways.

Long ago, when the first floods hit, the government began to prepare the mainland. Towering new cities were built high above the old, drowning ones. But out of sight is out of mind and they ignored us. And we let them. Self-contained and self-sufficient, we wrapped ourselves up in our island lives as if the flooding mainland were another world, nothing to do with us. We told ourselves that all the forecasts of doom were wrong, that it would never come to this. But it has. The sea has reached our very doorsteps and now, suddenly, it's too late.

Tain will stay on the island he's never left, not once, since the day he was born. All his memories and stories, all his knowledge, will sink with the island as it is gulped into the ocean.

As the boats pull away the old ones turn to the hills and we leave the island, like a bit of discarded litter, to the mercy of the North Sea.

The vast towers of Glasgow shimmer through morning mists as we pull across the expanse of sea that was once the rolling farmlands of Ayrshire. Days and nights in the murderous swells of the Atlantic have left us all sick and exhausted. I stretch as best I can in my cramped space and long to be still but there's no land or harbour to be seen, only a chaos of boats cluttering the waters around the tall metal walls that bar refugees from the city.

Like Tain, I'd never left the island. I'd never seen a city till now, never known a building higher than a cottage. I'd seen old newsreel of the seas rising and huge stretches of the waterlogged UK being turned into Eurostat fish farms. Our compulink teacher showed us a virtual reality simulation of the old city of Glasgow flooding and the new supraground structure rising block by block, growing in seconds on-screen into cloud-level tower blocks, linked by the connecting channels of the sky trains and crowned by the huge dome of the cyberspace centre that has made Glasgow one of the most prosperous of the new Information-trading cities.

But the reality of the supraground city that sits before me is a thousand times more awesome than any computer simulation. It is a monstrous, gleaming, strangely beautiful titanium web that towers high above the sea and fills the sky.

The chaos of the boat village is also much worse than we could have imagined. I scan the heaving mass of boats for my family but they could be anywhere. I can't bear to think that they might not be there at all.

A speedboat cuts across our path and I see guns glinting above the bow windscreen.

'Sea police. Heads down!' orders Alex, who looks wrecked after steering all night, down through what remains of the Western Isles.

The speedboat circles, its machine guns keeping us in their sights. A megaphone voice commands us to turn back but we row on – there's nowhere to turn back to. The sea police fire a volley of bullets overhead but Alex keeps his nerve.

All of a sudden the sea police about-turn and speed off. Alex steers us to a mooring place on the edge of the boat village that stretches far out into the waters around the city walls.

'Why didn't they shoot?' I ask him.

'What were they going to do – massacre us all?' Alex shakes his head as we gaze at the fishing boats, ferries, racing yachts, tiny pleasure cruisers, all kinds, even ramshackle handmade rafts with patchwork sails.

'Where are they all from?' I whisper.

'This is what's left of the population of Ayrshire,' says Alex. 'I've heard there's a fleet in from Northern Ireland, and the Western Isles are due to evacuate any day . . .' He trails off. The scale of this exodus is too much to take in.

'Alex,' says Kate, who is trying to cope with three hungry and restless young children. 'What about food and fresh water?'

Alex stares across the filthy, littered water to the city.

'There must be some kind of food supply system,' he says. 'They can't let us starve.'

'Of course they'll let us starve,' someone yells. 'We should have stayed on the island with the old folk, all together, where we belonged. We'll die anyway in these stinking waters.'

As Alex tries to steady the outburst of anger and panic I, too, wish that I had stayed on the drowning island, clutching Tain's sleeve as I did when I was little. Anything but this.

In the middle of the night there's a clamour like the end of the world. A great swarm of police speedboats and waterbikes is buzzing round the metal gates, lights flashing, sirens screaming. We keep our heads down as bullets fly and the gates slide open to let a ship enter. Reels of tide crash us into the next-door yacht and bedlam breaks out as a surge of boats makes a frantic dash in the ship's wake, through the sea police, towards the city gates.

'Why don't they just let us in? Doesn't anyone care?'

'Doubt it,' says Alex. 'These cities are for the elite, for the technology wizards. They only hold a finite number of people. We're surplus to requirements, not so much as a footnote on government policy. Just a social parasite clinging to the city walls, a form of pollution. I doubt if most of the people up there know much about what's going on down here. They sit up there with their heads in the clouds in those ivory towers, plugged into cyberspace. They can go on virtual reality holidays to every time and place in human history, they can access enough information to fill a universe, yet they don't know what's happening right under their noses.'

'They don't care,' I tell him. 'Why else build a city with barricades?'

Machine-gun fire has battered back most of the chancers; several boats have crashed or overturned; but two make it right through the city gates before they slide shut.

Alex meets my eyes.

'But it can be done,' I whisper. 'There *is* a way in.'

Days blur into a hell of nothingness. Only hunger and thirst and cold, and the overpowering sewage stench that rises from the water, convince me I'm still alive. Violence erupts whenever the Red Cross aid ship arrives to dish out scanty supplies of food and water – the surplus leftovers from the city.

Each morning I make a precarious journey around the boats, leaping from one to the other, searching for Mum, Dad and the two little ones. I try to map out the pattern of the sea village in my head, but each day new craft arrive and the pattern changes. It's impossible.

Yet I refuse to believe that my family is not here, somewhere, searching for me too.

On the fourth day hunger and despair get the better of me and a blanketing stupor descends that makes me huddle in the boat. When at last I rouse myself, I stare around with eyes and head so clear and sharp I feel I've crystallized into a shard of glass.

'It's the hunger,' Alex tells me. 'Hunger sharpens you like nothing else.'

I must use it, I tell myself. This hunger, this sharpness.

With my new sharp senses I focus in on the curious splashings around the thick legs of the sea-bridge that shuttles the sky trains out of the city to the airport built on the island of Arran, its mountain peaks still high above the sea.

'Water rats,' says Alex, following my gaze. 'Human water-rats.'

And I lean forward till I'm almost tipping out of the boat to watch the children who play around the great legs of the sea-bridge on metal bin lids, bathtubs, car tyres, old doors – all sorts of odd junk rafts and vessels.

At the blare of a police siren the water-rat children rush for the bridge legs like iron filings to a magnet, and disappear.

'The bridge legs, are they hollow?' I ask Alex.

'Must be, unless those kids are magicians.'

I'm smiling, though I'm not sure why. But it's the first beat of life, the only spark of hope I've known since we left the drowning island; a spark lit by the strange idea that there might be a warren of water-rat children surviving in the hollow legs of the sea-bridge.

Later, I watch as one of the children skids skilfully across the waves on a bin-lid raft, like a cherub in a tin can. He spins and flits, playing with the waves, practising manoeuvres. When he crashes out of a spin and laughs, I find I'm laughing too.

'Not water-rats,' I tell Alex. 'Sea-urchins, that's what they are.'

Sun burns on the glass and metal web that meshes the sky above our heads. My flicker of hope flames into a sudden bright image of a life up in the supraground city, where there is no hunger or cold or filth or disease. I will not stay in this floating nightmare any longer, I tell myself. I must act. I must find my family and get into the city. We'll find work and make a life up there in that gleaming web.

'Let's get out of this, Alex,' I plead. 'We'll all die right here if we stay put.'

Already, there is sickness on our boat. In just a week Alex has shrivelled to an old man, so weary with defeat he seems older than Tain.

'We're jam-packed,' he mutters. 'There's no way out. Even if there was, there's a firing squad waiting.'

His words skim off me as I watch the sea-urchins make more reckless dashes from their hideouts in the bridge legs to the metal jaws of the city gates. I'm keeping score. Umpteen near misses, three shot down and nine in. Better odds than staying here and catching the sickness that is spreading round the boats.

At daybreak I fasten my few belongings about me and step across the huddled bodies, then leap to the next boat and the next. It takes several days to make a complete circuit of the city walls. I shout for Mum and Dad till I'm hoarse, ask for my family on every boat I board, scanning each face as I jump, aching for a glimpse of a hand or a clump of hair that is as familiar as my own.

Exhaustion eventually grinds me to a stop. I could spend the rest of my life in this useless, circling quest. Surely, if my family were here, we would have found each other by now. They would have made their own search for me.

'Tell me, Alex,' I plead, once I locate my own boat again, 'I need to know. Do you think they made it?'

Alex sighs beneath his blanket. At last he concedes, 'I don't think they did.' He turns his head. 'You're young and bright and strong, Mara. You might just make it.'

He huddles back under his blanket and I stand, aimless and desolate. Once upon a time I felt young and bright and strong, but not now. I jump boats again until I'm at the outermost edge of the boat village. Dark, empty sea lies before me; a sea that has swallowed up the people I love. Why take them and leave me? I ask. And as I stand, wretched and angry, in front of that lonely sea I want to throw myself into it and join them.

Then, out of nowhere, I seem to hear a voice, as soft and distinct as the slap of water on the boats. Tain's voice.

Go now, Mara. Go and find a new future.

I pause for just a moment and listen to the sounds

of the sea-urchins splashing around the bridge legs. When I jump into the filthy sea I'm not sure whether it's because I want to live or die.

The water is so numbingly cold it turns my body to rubber in seconds but I swim frantically until I reach the great legs of the sea-bridge. Instantly, I'm surrounded by a clattering, crashing wave of sea-urchins. They spin around me on their tyres, bin lids, plastic bathtubs and old doors. They splash in my face, prodding and tormenting until I begin to drift into exhaustion, slipping down towards a numb, safe place.

Suddenly my hair is yanked, hard, and the pain rouses me. I thrash out, grab the edge of something solid and find I'm face to face with a tiny urchin in an upturned car bonnet. He sits in it like a muddy oyster in an open shell, baby-faced, with dangerous eyes, paddling with an upended street sign. The skin of his unclothed body is sleek with mud and slime.

I gasp, trying to loosen his grip on my hair. The urchin leans towards me.

'Let go!' I yell. 'Listen to me. I want to get into the city.'

He listens intently, but there is a blankness in his eyes that tells me he doesn't understand. Frantically, I gesture to myself then to the city, trying to keep calm as the other urchins continue to bash and prod me with their makeshift vessels and paddles, splashing the scummy water in my eyes and mouth.

The urchin in the car bonnet makes an urgent sound

and almost chokes me in his effort to snap off my neck-lace – a leather thong Tain made for me that's hung with a piece of quartz he found on the island.

'Take it,' I tell him, and he yelps with joy as I slip the necklace over my head and give it to him. I clamber aboard his metal raft. 'Now take me to the city.'

He pats me once or twice as if I'm a stray pet he has picked up out of the water, chuckles, then paddles out to the bridge leg that is closest to the city gates. Then we wait.

From time to time the urchin touches the quartz stone he's tied around his skinny waist, as if he thinks it holds a kind of magic. Deep into the night, when I've grown used to the rubbery numbness of my cold body, the metal bridge leg beside us begins to vibrate with sound. The urchin's eyes gleam and he fastens my fingers to the rim of our vessel and pushes me flat. When I protest he bites me, viciously, on the arm.

I am in charge, the child's eyes and his bite tell me.

When the supply ship draws close, we move. The urchin paddles furiously and we spin faster and faster towards the city. Machine-gun fire is close and relentless. I look up and see the sheer surface of a metal gate stretching high into the night sky. We spin past it, churned in the foaming wake of the supply ship.

Then, at long last, we are still. But there's no time to let the dizziness and sickness settle.

'Over there, quick!' I tell the urchin. The supra-ground lift gleams across the water, a gold-plated capsule ready to ascend out of this hell.

Beside me, the child lies unmoving. There is a dark streak of blood washing across his face and a gash in the side of his head. A bullet or a collision with the metal gates? In a panic, I feel for his pulse as I look towards the low platform that leads to the lift capsule. If I paddled over I could pull myself up onto it. Workers from the supply ship are cramming in and it would be easy to slip among them, unnoticed. I could make it if I go now.

But if I go now I will abandon the child with a gash in his head and a dodgy pulse beat. The urchin who risked his life to get me here.

As I rip off the sleeve of my shirt to stem the gush of blood from the child's head, the lift doors buzz shut and the golden capsule ascends to the supraground web.

Desolate, I paddle through the dark of the old drowned city. Aimlessly, we drift. After some time the urchin sits up and grunts.

'Speak,' I plead with him, but he stares at me, word-less.

I peel off the blood-soaked bandage to have a look at his head. The blood still pours and he is as pale as a ghost but it must be a surface wound or he wouldn't be sitting up. I groan, realizing I missed my chance on the supraground lift to be landed with a grunting sea-urchin.

The urchin grunts again, urgently, and gestures at something in front of us. I peer into the deep shadows cast over the sea city by the massive supraground structure, and see a great darkness rising from the water.

'What is it?' I ask. The child explodes into excited grunts and squeals, gesturing us onwards towards the dark shadow. As we draw closer, I see what it is: a hump of land. The urchin knows something of this place, I'm sure, but he can't tell me.

When the raft knocks against the land, we climb out. I reach down and touch grass. A large building sits on the hilltop and some soft, flickering glow lights it from within. The urchin has erupted in a delighted, word-less babble.

'It's a church,' I tell him as I recognize the solid, familiar outline. But as we draw close and I see the scale of the building I know it's no ordinary church, abandoned on this green hilltop. It's Glasgow's ancient cathedral.

The child pulls me through its heavy, wooden doors and I gasp. The vast hall of the cathedral is lit with candles and swarms with a mass of dirt-caked, naked urchins. They perch on high window ledges, squabble upon tombstones, scamper and squeal among the massive pillars.

A cathedral full of water-rat children! It would make Alex laugh; the old, madcap Alex I remember from the island. But my eyes are filling with tears as I look at these abandoned little creatures who have

21

made a chaotic haven of this ancient place. My tears are hot with anger at a city of people who could do this, who have no thought or care for anyone outside, not even for children. Not for these orphaned urchins or for my own lost brother and sister.

My urchin looks up at me and smiles. I wipe my eyes and lift a lock of his long, mud-packed hair to examine his head wound in the light of a torch flame. 'You'll live,' I tell him.

He stares at me, then points up at my face.

'Mara,' I tell him. 'My name is Mara.'

The urchin touches his own face and looks at me, intense and wondering. Underneath the mud and slime I see for the first time that his body has a sleek covering of hair. The hair of a water-rat. They all have. I shudder, then make myself reach out and touch him because he's just a little child really. An abandoned little one.

'You've no name, have you?' I ask him. 'Never mind, I'll give you a name.'

No parents, no name, no language. It would be a huge task, trying to look after these urchins, teaching them to speak. But the very thought begins to ease the terrible guilt that has been churning inside me: guilt at surviving when the ones I love did not.

'Are you my future?' I murmur to the sea-urchin, as I look around at the hundreds of little human water-rats, this strange new amphibian race that is surviving, unknown, on the ancient hilltop remains of the drowned city.

There was nothing I could do to save Tain or my family but maybe I can do something for these lost little ones. Maybe I can be a big sister to them. It would be something to live for.

Outside, the waters of the sea city flicker with the lights cast by the supraground web above our heads. I gaze up at its crowning metal dome and try to imagine all those people, absorbed in their virtual reality worlds, endlessly shopping for information and holidaying in cyberspace, filling up their lives with things that are exotic and exciting, useless and unreal.

Aching hunger and cold are my reality. It's the reality of this cathedral full of urchins. I look out into the deep shadows that lie between the glistening reflections on the water and when daybreak comes I'm still sitting on the cathedral hilltop.

Out of the morning mist I watch as six, seven, eight islands, topped with trees and ruins, slowly emerge. They lie unguarded, unpoliced, forgotten.

And as I look at them I try to imagine a future that is built on the old ways; a new world that cares for its people as we did on the island. But one that is not a world unto itself, selfish and careless of what lies beyond it, as the supraground city is. As we on the island were too, in our way.

Maybe there is some kind of future I can build for

myself and the sea-urchins; a savage future, yet one that is more human than the supraground web that clutters the sky above my head. Maybe we can begin a better new world on these green, forgotten islands that lie among the risen waters of the old city.

SEIZE THE FIRE
by Mary Hoffman

Toke placed his feet as carefully as he could on the forest floor. But, as quiet as each step was on the damp leaves, he knew that his walk was being paced by even softer footfalls. Every now and again he would stop and listen, but all he could hear was the thumping of his own heart and the distant chittering of monkeys and birds.

It was getting dark and soon it would be impossible to see the path without a torch. But it was warm and muggy as only a tropical forest can be. There would be many more hours before the cool of the middle of the night. And then he heard it. One single cough, alarmingly close. He had been right about the silent stalker. The tiger was there.

Toke froze, not daring to lower his foot for the next

step. He turned his head slowly towards the direction of the cough. The dying light caught its reflection in two amber eyes in the bushes. A dark shape, brindled with deeper shadows, flowed towards Toke in one easy bound. He felt the hot breath, smelt the tawny tang of big cat and then—

GAME OVER, blinked the message on his goggles.

Toke took off his helmet, sighed and stretched. He had never got any further than this with 'Wild Tiger', sometimes not so far. Most kids played the game because, if you could get to the end of the forest trail before dark without the tiger detecting your presence, you would get an amazing number of credit points on your card – enough to buy your own virtual reality game. Toke played because he wanted to see a tiger.

See it, not smell it or feel its hot breath just before it devoured you. Creep so cautiously that you could circle round behind it and watch it before it saw you. There were other VR programs, of course, the educational ones, but none of them had wild tigers.

And Toke didn't need those programs, not any more. He knew everything there was to know about tigers and had been in love with the big striped cats ever since he was a very small boy. But he had never seen a real one.

In the nineteenth and twentieth centuries there were still tigers all over India and Nepal and Sumatra and Siberia. But by the end of the second millennium there were hardly any left. The rugs and stuffed heads and luxury coats had taken their toll, followed by poachers who sold bones and bits of tiger for medicine and magic.

In 1998 someone had suggested that the problem of tigers in the wild couldn't be solved and that the only way to save tigers was to farm them and kill some of the farmed animals for their body parts. It caused international outrage, but by 2010 it was a fact; the tiger farms began, followed by the elephant and rhino farms.

People were still uneasy about it but the farms were not illegal. At the same time conservation projects took the place of zoos. They were not open to the public but they were devoted to the ideal of looking after large mammals until their natural habitats could be regenerated.

The only zoo Toke had visited was a virtual one, where remaining footage of large mammals was supplemented by computer enhancement and digital tricks. Toke had stroked a tiger in his virtual zoo, but it didn't satisfy him. Nothing would do that except coming face to face with a real tiger. And that was hard to do in 2030.

A yowling from outside his sleep unit door roused Toke from his thoughts. He got up and opened the door and in walked his own private tiger, Geronimo, the closest thing to a wild cat Toke knew. He scooped her up in his arms and sat on the bed while the cat rubbed her cheek against his, telling him how much she loved him with her low rumbling purr.

Just then Toke's mum burst in, gesturing excitedly at the wall where his computer screen was. 'There's an e-mail for you, Toke,' she said. 'From the Global Animal Conservation Trust.'

Toke held his breath. He had entered a competition to win a trip to India, to visit the Tiger Project Centre. He had written a long essay about the future importance of regenerating wild habitats, using all his knowledge and love of tigers to add force to his arguments. Toke turned on his screen and read the message without taking it in.

'Congratulations,' said Mum, reading over his shoulder. 'You won! You'll see your tiger at last.'

Geronimo didn't like all the rushing round over the next few weeks. Mum had to organize time off from her software firm so that she could go with Toke, and he had to get permission to have a week off school. Bags were packed and unpacked. Just how hot would it be in India?

At last Toke and his mum boarded the hover-shuttle to the airport, leaving Dad with many instructions about feeding and caring for the cat. The supersonic flight took four hours and they stepped out into brilliant sunshine and stifling heat. They were grateful to climb into the air-conditioned shuttle that took them to the Tiger Project Centre.

The buildings, including the guest rooms for visitors, were underground and naturally cool. Toke and his mum had adjoining rooms with a sliding door between them. They had nothing to do that first night except meet their host, Dr Greenstreet, the director of the centre. He was a tall, thin man with glasses and the first person Toke had ever met who knew more about tigers than he did.

As Toke lay in his comfortable bed, he thought, I'm in India; but it was hard to believe. His imagination, fuelled by history video-clips, summoned up a tent, a camp-bed, a mosquito net, and the night sounds of the jungle. But in fact he could hear nothing but the whirr of the controlled temperature and humidity unit.

Next morning Dr Greenstreet took Toke on a tour of the centre, beginning with its substantial research facility. Here scientists worked on stored tiger DNA, artificial insemination, diet, diseases and anything else that could affect captive tigers. When Toke thought he couldn't take another laboratory, he was led up a spiral staircase out into the natural light. The sunshine made him blink and his heart was beating fast. He was going to see his first tiger.

It was the smell which reached him first. Not just the musky big-cat smell, familiar from countless virtual reality programs, but the smell of the natural outside world, which he rarely met. The sun beat down on the compound and the trees around it were full of brightly coloured birds and rustlings of small mammals.

Dr Greenstreet took Toke down a shady corridor roofed with plaited bamboo.

'How many tigers are there?' asked Toke.

'About thirty adults and half a dozen cubs at any one time. They are all kept very healthy, because of their regulated diet and our vaccination programme. They're in much better shape than they would be in the wild.'

'But you will return them to the wild as soon as you can, won't you?' asked Toke.

For a moment he thought Dr Greenstreet was going to say no; he seemed to prefer having tigers where he could keep an eye on them. But he quickly smiled and said, 'Of course. But it will take a long time for regeneration to be complete. So much jungle was cleared for agriculture in the late twentieth century.'

Dr Greenstreet punched a code into a computerized door lock at the end of the corridor.

Another worker behind them had been listening. She smiled at Toke. She was a young woman with short curly red hair and freckles. 'But it will happen, Peter,' she said to Dr Greenstreet.

'Ah, Halley,' he said, 'I didn't see you. Will you take over and show our guest the animals? I really should get back to the lab.'

'Sure,' said Halley, taking Toke through the heavy door.

When they were on the other side, she looked at him for a long time before asking, 'What do you think of the centre so far?'

'It makes me want to puke!' said Toke, and then

turned bright red, surprised by his own reaction. But he couldn't stop. 'OK, the tigers are well looked after, I guess. And they might be extinct in the wild if you didn't have places like this. But how can you love tigers and be happy to keep them in cages and runs instead of working flat out to get them back into the wild?'

'You do love tigers, don't you?' said Halley softly. She put her hand on Toke's shoulder. 'Come and see them before you say any more.'

She led Toke, still trembling from his outburst, down a metal-lined corridor with bolted doors on either side and then back out into the bright sunshine. And there they were.

Pacing up and down in their separate metal-fenced runs, the big cats swung their tails and shook their heads. Their glossy coats shone and their white teeth flashed as they snarled with every turn. Halley took Toke slowly along the runs, naming all the tigers: Sheba, Solomon, Tariq, Taahra, Yasmin and her cubs, Rafi the two-year-old.

Rafi was a magnificent specimen, a great advertisement for the centre's health claims. As he reached the bars nearest to Toke, he shook his head and made a snuffling noise, a cross between a sneeze and a grunt.

Halley looked quickly both ways to check that there was no-one else in the compound and led Toke to the middle, away from the fences. 'Look,' she said under her breath, 'I shouldn't tell you this, but everything isn't quite what it seems at this centre. I can't talk freely.

There are bugs on the gates and CCTV cameras filming everything. Pretend I'm pointing out the security devices to you. Have you been to the computer suite yet?'

'I'm going to get a tour this afternoon,' said Toke, mystified.

'It's a slim chance they'll leave you on your own, but try to find a file called "Investments".'

'What does that mean?' asked Toke. It didn't sound very exciting.

'You'll see,' said Halley grimly. 'Use the password "Farmer". Have you got something you could down-load the file onto?'

'Yes,' said Toke. 'I've got my pocketbook.'

'Good,' said Halley. 'That'll be very useful to us.'

'Who's "us"?'

'I can't tell you more now, but I'll meet you in the VR room after dinner.'

Just then another worker with a clipboard came out into the compound and pressed a series of buttons which released the calorie-controlled vitamin-enriched tiger food into the animals' feeding areas. Toke went back into the metal corridor and through the security door into the bamboo one.

It was a relief to find his mother waiting for him on the other side. But they were taken to lunch by the director and Toke couldn't tell her everything about his morning. He ate his lunch almost in silence, but his mother was enthusiastic enough for both of them. 'I've been talking to your head of Information Services,' she said. 'I think we could provide you with some software to speed up your data exchange with other centres.'

The computer suite was next to the labs. A white-coated programmer showed Toke around, demonstrating the state-of-the-art hardware and software. All the tiger projects around the world used a high-speed link to communicate to one another and data was shared once it had been collected. But Toke's mother was sure she could cut seconds off the transfer and was deep in discussion with one of the researchers.

'Choose a tiger,' said Toke's programmer; 'one of the ones you saw this morning.'

'Rafi,' said Toke quickly.

R-A-F-I, typed the programmer. 'There we are!'

The tiger's face filled the screen, every stripe and whisker in sharp definition.

'You can access his height and weight at any date in his history, plus his blood type, DNA structure, his diet, his vaccinations, anything you want to know,' said the programmer, 'and so can any of our colleagues at the other centres.'

He let Toke scroll and click his way through all the data. At the bottom was a box he didn't understand – FORECAST. He clicked on it. The screen bore a single date – 12 June – tomorrow.

'What does that mean?' asked Toke.

The programmer looked at him anxiously. 'You

don't need to worry about that. Why don't you look up our records on cubs?'

Just then something started beeping on the lapel of his white coat. 'Excuse me a moment.' He took out a communicator and engaged in a brief conversation. 'Would you mind if I left you on your own for a few minutes? You seem to have picked up the basics. You can carry on looking things up while I'm away.'

Toke put on his politest smile and said he'd be fine. He couldn't believe his luck. FIND FILE. INVESTMENTS, he typed. CLASSIFIED. TOP SECURITY, read the screen; ENTER PASSWORD. FARMER, typed in Toke and was greeted with the message ACCESS GRANTED. As the screen filled up with data on animals and a list of dates, Toke's blood ran cold. There were columns with entries like 'tailbone', 'ribs' and 'skin', with large sums of money beside them. This wasn't a conservation centre at all. It was a cover-up for a tiger farm!

At the bottom of the list was tomorrow's date and the name RAFI. Toke couldn't believe it. Rafi would be killed tomorrow and his beautiful body cut up and sold for profit. Whose profit? Dr Greenstreet's probably. Toke wondered how many other workers at the centre knew about it – Halley, obviously, but she clearly wasn't on Greenstreet's side. Perhaps she could do something to save Rafi?

Toke hastily got out his pocketbook and began to transfer the data. He had just finished and changed the open file by the time the programmer returned. 'I hope you don't mind,' he said. 'I copied some data to use when I write up my report for school.'

The programmer looked at the screen: CARNIVORE DIET, FELID FORMULA. 'That's fine, Toke,' he said.

Halley was waiting for him in the VR room. 'Did you find it?' she whispered.

Toke nodded. 'It's in my pocketbook,' he said. 'Is it safe to talk?'

'Put on this helmet and goggles. If we stand at these two consoles, the CCTV cameras won't know we aren't playing and our intelligence says this room isn't bugged.'

'Who's "us"?' Toke asked for the second time and got a full answer.

It was the weirdest experience of his life, standing next to Halley in a VR helmet listening to her soft voice pour out a crazy story of greed and corruption in high places and an underground movement dedicated to sabotage and the liberation of tigers.

'Noah's Army, that's what we're called. We've liberated twenty tigers from farms, including this so-called conservation project, in the last eighteen months. We can't save them all, of course, or we'd give ourselves away. It has to look like an accident every time.'

'What happens to them afterwards?' asked Toke.

'Eight were shot,' said Halley. 'It's a risk every time. But some of us work outside the farms. We're trying to re-establish the tigers in the wild and to breed enough to make these obscene farms obsolete.'

'Is there anywhere safe for them to live?' asked Toke.

'Yes, one of the regeneration projects is only a few miles from here and the director is sympathetic to Noah's Army. Her own brother is one of our agents.'

'But isn't what you do very dangerous?'

'Incredibly,' said Halley, and Toke could hear she was grinning. 'We are all crazy, what with the risks of being caught in the farms, and the risks of handling tigers on our own. Of course, the operation here is pretty unusual. We usually liberate tigers from the known farms.'

'Can't you tell someone about Greenstreet and stop him?'

'We were working on that. It was my job to get the data off that "Investments" file, so that we had proof. Thanks to you, we've got that now. But the news about Rafi changes everything. There's no time to get the information to the proper authorities in time to save him. We'll have to carry out an emergency rescue.'

'How?'

Halley didn't answer straight away. Instead she said, 'Toke, have you wondered why I'm telling you all this?'

Toke felt the hairs on his neck rise as he realized he knew the answer. 'You want me to help.'

'One of our key members is sick with a fever. There's no time to get anyone else infiltrated and there's no-one I can trust in the centre. It'll take two

36

of us on the inside and at least three on the outside to spring a tiger. It's a lot to ask, but will you step in and help me liberate Rafi?'

'Why me?' asked Toke.

'I think you know,' said Halley. 'It's only people who really love tigers who can be part of Noah's Army.'

It was what Toke wanted to hear but he still couldn't believe it. His brain was in a whirl but there was no time to think it over. 'When?' he whispered.

'Tonight,' said Halley. 'Two o'clock. Here's what we'll do.'

Toke's mother was sure he was coming down with something. 'You've hardly said a word all day and I thought you'd be just buzzing with all those tigers you've seen and everything you've found out.' She insisted on giving him a mediscan and was almost disappointed to discover that his temperature and blood pressure were normal.

'It's OK, Mum,' said Toke. 'I think I'm just tired. You know, it's been a lot to take in. I think I'll get an early night.'

That is a line which always works with mums. She yawned in sympathy. 'Good idea. I think I'll do the same. Being on holiday is so tiring.'

Toke smiled. Mum put in sixteen-hour days at home running her own software business, and she was entitled to a holiday. But instead of sightseeing, she had spent the whole day talking computers with the staff at the centre; she was exhausted: convenient for Toke's first mission with Noah's Army.

At first he thought he'd never do more than doze. But the computer beeped him into wakefulness from a deep sleep. It was one thirty in the morning. He slipped on his shoes and quietly opened his door. The corridor was empty, but shone with a dim green light. Toke found his way to the spiral staircase and crept up and out into the cold night air.

He shivered as he walked down the bamboo corridor, wishing he was wearing something warmer than T-shirt and shorts. When he punched in the code Halley had given him, each beep sounded eerily loud. He slipped through the metal door and froze as a hand grabbed his arm. 'Halley?' he hissed. 'You nearly gave me a heart attack!'

'Sorry,' whispered Halley. 'You got here earlier than I thought you would. The perimeter guards are just passing.'

They waited about three minutes, then slipped out into the compound. The moonlight shone on several tigers, turning their gold bars to silver.

'The farmed tigers are often restless the night before a cull,' whispered Halley. 'We think they sense it.'

'You've done this yourself before?' asked Toke.

'Once or twice,' grinned Halley. 'I've been an inside agent on two farms but this is the first tiger I've liberated from this centre. And I had to get the team together so fast I'm not sure if I've covered all my tracks. So I'm out of here as soon as Rafi is safe.'

Rafi was awake. He lifted his head at their approach and sniffed the air. Then he came up to the bars of his run and made the snuffle of greeting.

'Don't worry, Rafi,' Toke told him. 'We're going to get you out.'

'Remember what I told you, Toke,' warned Halley. 'He's still a big dangerous meat-eater, not a pussycat. Never stop being afraid, or you could make a serious mistake.'

Toke heard a low whistle from the outer fence and knew that there were other members of Noah's Army out there. It made him feel braver than he really was. But there was no disguising that this was the most dangerous thing he had ever done. And, unlike the others, he was only a kid.

The next few moments were crucial. Halley had organized a 'power failure', which would immobilize the cameras, microphones and alarm system for about ten minutes. She was going to open Rafi's door and the gate in the perimeter fence. She knew the combinations, of course, but had to make it look as if it were linked to the fluctuation in the power supply. The outside team was going to accept Rafi as soon as he was out. But getting the tiger out was a two-person job, which was where Toke came in.

'Ready?' asked Halley.

Toke nodded.

She punched the combination into the lock on Rafi's cage and released the door, then held it in place. Rafi was just on the other side.

'Quick, hold the door while I release the gate,' said Halley.

Toke put his weight against the door, wedging it almost but not quite shut. He looked into Rafi's eyes while Halley dealt with the outer gate. Then they swapped places, with Toke holding the outside gate, while Halley prepared to release the tiger.

She nodded to Toke in the moonlight. He whistled softly twice to the waiting team, to signal that the time had come. Then he opened the gate outwards into the jungle. A split second later Halley opened Rafi's door and called him out.

The tiger moved cautiously out of his run. The outside team had brought meat with them to lure him towards the gate and he caught the aroma. Slowly he paced across the compound to the outer fence, ignoring Halley, who had closed in behind him to block his retreat.

Toke held his breath. The huge head lifted and Rafi looked him in the eyes once more. Then the sinuous black and gold body slipped past him and out of the gate, so close that the tiger's fur brushed his bare legs. Rafi had escaped.

But in that moment of triumph, Toke's exultation turned to terror as he heard the sound of people in the metal corridor.

Halley froze for a second, then did the unthinkable. She thrust Toke out into the night. 'Hide!' she hissed.

There was no time for further explanation. Toke hid.

From behind the bushes outside the compound he could hear voices – several male voices – raised in anger, then Halley's, calm and explanatory. Suddenly an ear-piercing alarm went off and bright searchlights flashed on all along the perimeter fence. Toke had to move fast. Guards were rushing to the gate from both inside and outside the fence. Toke turned and ran.

He ran until he had a stitch, then stopped, doubled up, to get his breath back. The shouts from the centre had faded and he was deep in the heart of the jungle. He had no idea where he was. And then suddenly he recognized it.

He was on a path just like the one in 'Wild Tiger'. He inched his way soundlessly along, sure that another, softer footfall was matching him pace for pace. Was it Rafi? Halley had told him that another tiger liberated from this centre, Rukhshana, was living in the regenerated habitat nearby. They hoped that Rafi would mate with her and that she would bring two or three cubs to adulthood in the wild. Suppose Rukhshana had wandered close to the centre? If his silent companion was the tigress, she wouldn't know him. Did a love of tigers show in the dark? Toke wondered.

Then he heard a tiger cough. Oh God, I know how the next bit goes, thought Toke, expecting the rush of air, the hot stinking breath and then extinction. Only this time it would be for real.

But it wasn't 'Wild Tiger'. The tiger came towards him down the path and, after a few seconds of sheer terror, Toke saw that it was Rafi and that he had a large piece of raw meat in his jaws. Behind him came three people in camouflage fatigues, two men and a woman.

The people stopped in their tracks but Rafi came on. As he approached Toke, he paused and gave his snuffling grunt, muffled by the meat. Toke grunted back and the members of Noah's Army relaxed. 'You must be Toke,' said one of the men. 'What happened back there? Is Halley OK?'

'I don't know,' said Toke. 'Some people came into the tiger compound and she shoved me out of the gate. I heard them talking to her but then all hell broke loose and I just ran.'

There was a quick consultation, then the man said, 'I'll take you back and get you into the centre. Then I'll see if I can get Halley out. The others can look after Rafi till we rejoin them.'

They crept back through the jungle, Keti, as he was called, leading Toke round to the other side of the centre. There were no guards at the front; all their attention was directed to where animals might get out, not people in. Keti knew the security overrides and soon opened the door to the sleeping quarters.

'Go carefully, Toke,' he whispered. 'And well done. You've made a great start in the Army, releasing your first tiger. You're our youngest member ever. We'll be in touch.'

'See you,' said Toke. He stood for a while in the corridor, adjusting his eyes to the green light. He was bracing himself to get back into his room, hoping that the alarms hadn't wakened his mother. Bracing himself, too, for whatever had happened to Halley.

But whatever happened, he was now a member of Noah's Army. He had released his first tiger. And of one thing he was sure: it was not going to be the last.

WALKING THE WIRE
by Rhiannon Lassiter

Sagiko was late for class again. Transport in Tubetown
almost never ran on time and she'd had to wait almost
an hour this morning. Rain battered against the grimy
windows of the CityCrawler as it rumbled forward
another few metres. By squinting through the rain-
streaked window, Sagiko could see that the streets were
locked with Crawlers, moving ponderously through
the morning smog. Craning her neck and squinting
upwards, she could see the MechBirds outlined against
the grey sky as they soared past the crawling traffic.
Beside her, Tammy heaved a sigh and Sagiko knew she
was thinking how much faster she could get to school
if her family could afford a MechBird. Sagiko looked
away from the window. Like Tammy, she rode the
CityCrawler because it was free, but she didn't see any

point in wasting wishes on the impossible. Instead she opened one of the thick books she carried, hoping she wouldn't get a demerit for lateness if she scored high enough on the morning's test.

'Why do you bother?' Tammy asked. 'We'll have missed the test by now and we'll get a demerit for that as well as for being late.'

'We've only missed the first half,' Sagiko pointed out, without lifting her eyes from the book.

'You won't pass with half marks,' Tammy informed her and turned back to looking out of the window.

Sagiko, her lips moving silently as she revised for the test, didn't even hear her.

All Tammy carried was a hand–held datapad. Like Sagiko, she lived in Tubetown, but her parents had thrown all their resources into buying her a better future. They couldn't provide the kind of advantages Corptowners could afford, but they had saved to buy her an expensive computer to work on at home – although Tammy complained that, with the noise her younger brothers and sisters made, it was impossible to do homework. Sagiko's mother couldn't afford to do that, but she brought home old books from the Tubetown markets, easy to afford now that the libraries were becoming computerized and dumping their old stock. Sympathizing with Sagiko, the only other girl in her class to come from the tubes, Tammy would help her carry the stack to school, although the other children laughed at the heavy volumes with their dusty

pages. Tammy was embarrassed but Sagiko took no notice. Her books were just as useful as their datapads, even if they were hard to carry.

Five minutes later the Crawler ground to a halt again, but this time the hydraulics hissed as the doors opened. Grabbing the stack of books, the girls headed out into the rain. It stung their eyes as they pushed forward, the wind tugging at the flapping corners of their wet coats, towards the sign five metres ahead which read: TUBE 7-82. Struggling on, they reached the tube, its curved walls sprayed with the graffi-tags of rival gangs and its floor smeared with rainwater and dirt. From here it was another ten-minute walk through the intersections of Tubetown until they reached the gleaming heights of the school building.

The District Seven Special School was a gleaming white starscraper rising like a candle from the grime of Tubetown. Sagiko shook the worst of the rain from her coat before showing her school pass to the gate guards. The guards ran her pass and Tammy's through the computer slot, logging them as forty-five minutes late, before waving them through. The corridors were quiet as the girls made their way to the elevator; everyone else was already in class. Sagiko walked as fast as she could but Tammy lagged behind, fumbling in her pocket for something. She had to run to catch up before the elevator doors closed, almost dropping her heavy load of books. Two of them slithered out of her hands as she jumped past the closing doors and Sagiko bent to help pick them up. As she did so, she caught sight of the small white foil packet Tammy was clutching in her hand. She didn't mention it. Instead she piled the books up and turned to look out of the transparent walls of the elevator as it carried them high up the side of the school building. Through the clear crystal she could see the dark city beneath them with a clarity impossible through the smogged windows of the Crawler.

The school, like all of District Seven, was part of Corptown. Gleaming arcologies owned by rich corporations ran the transportation, provided health care and education and arranged the entertainment. Everything was for the benefit of their employees, but the lucky few, like Tammy and Sagiko, could win scholarships, giving them the precious pass into Corptown and out of the tubes. From the elevator Sagiko could see the line where the immaculate arcologies were replaced by crumbling old brick and stone buildings and newer, slab-like concrete units already covered in graffi-tags. She felt guilty because leaving Tubetown seemed like an escape. She always did. Despite the crime and the poverty, with no corps to enforce the law or care for the citizens, it was still her home. To long for the clean heights of Corptown felt like disloyalty.

The elevator came smoothly to a halt and Sagiko turned away from the view of the city to the opening doors. Tammy had half turned away from her, crushing the piece of white foil into a ball and shoving it into her pocket. Sagiko pretended not to see and headed out of the elevator. Now wasn't the time to ask questions. Their classroom was only a few doors down. A polished sign on the door proclaimed it to be:

YEAR 12: CLASSROOM 3
STREAM 1: ALPHA
ADVANCED

Sagiko knocked softly on the door before entering, Tammy close behind. The class teacher looked up from her desk at the front of the class. The wall screen behind her displayed the words TEST PERIOD: 1 HOUR. The rest of the class were working silently at the computer terminals, although a few heads turned as the late-comers entered. The teacher frowned and waved them to their desks before touching a few keys on her own terminal. As Sagiko reached her desk and slid as quietly as she could into her chair the screen in front of her came to life with the words: MISSED 47 MINUTES TEST PERIOD: 1 DEMERIT.

Silently, Sagiko piled her books on the floor and entered the computer code that would begin the test. With only fifteen minutes left, she had no hope of scoring highly, but passing would prevent her from earning a third demerit. She focused her concentration on the softly glowing screen, deliberately forgetting the misfortunes of the morning in an effort to think of nothing but the questions in front of her. As usual they were difficult, and she had no time to give long answers. Instead she tried to express herself as succinctly as possible, keeping her answers short and as accurate as she knew how. She had answered just over half of them when the teacher stood up and signalled an end to the test period. The questions and answers disappeared from Sagiko's screen, to be automatically graded by the teacher's computer. Sitting back in her chair she tried to relax and glanced around the rest of the classroom. Some of the other children were looking anxious, reaching for their datapads to check their answers; others smiled confidently.

The girl two seats in front of Sagiko was turning to talk quietly to her friends, her casual attitude showing that the test had caused her no problems. Sagiko ignored her; the girl's name was Charlotte and she was Wired, her intelligence and memory boosted by expensive medical surgery. Only people who lived in Corptown could afford to have their children Wired. Sagiko had studied half the night in the small CityWarren room she shared with her mother. She tried not to think that Charlotte would not have needed to study for more than an hour to pass this test.

The results were coming in: the pupils' names appeared on the large wall screen, with their results next to them. Charlotte was at the top of the list with 100 per cent, followed by the other six children in the class who were Wired, all scoring over 95 per cent.

Sagiko scanned down the list for her name and found it at the very bottom. She had scored 56 per cent, just enough to pass. Concerned that Tammy might have failed, she looked for her friend's name and blinked when she saw it. Tammy was in the top ten, with a score of 89 per cent. Sagiko turned to the desk on her right to congratulate her but Tammy wasn't looking at her. Her eyes were fixed on the main screen and Sagiko was shocked to see how pale she looked. She reached out to touch her friend's arm and Tammy jumped as if an electric shock had gone through her.

'Are you all right?' Sagiko asked quietly.

'I'm fine,' Tammy said quickly. She gave Sagiko a small tight smile. 'Bet you didn't think I'd pass.'

'You did very well,' Sagiko replied. 'Congratulations. You must have studied hard.'

Tammy looked sideways at her and smiled secretively. 'There's more to life than studying,' she said smugly. 'You have to be clever to get the marks.'

Sagiko looked away, embarrassed. She concentrated on her own score. She had answered every question right and it hadn't been her fault that she had had no time to finish. But Sagiko's intelligence had earned her the school pass into Corptown. Without that pass she'd have to go to a charity school or start work. She was scared to think that she might not deserve it and resolved to work all the harder. She spent her first free period redoing the test and satisfying herself that she would have scored much higher marks if she'd had the time to complete it. The teacher wouldn't care about that but it made Sagiko feel better. She spent the rest of her free time, including her lunch break, reading ahead on her computer for tomorrow's class. Usually she ate lunch with Tammy, but today Tammy was hanging around Charlotte and her friends, trying to get them to talk to her. Sagiko could see that Charlotte thought Tammy was a joke and was only paying her attention in order to laugh at her. But Tammy desperately wanted to be like Charlotte and she still hoped that the Corptown girls would be her friends and invite her back to their homes or give her a lift in their parents' MechBirds. Sagiko would normally have ignored Tammy's behaviour, knowing that her friend would come back when Charlotte got bored of her, but today she was worried about her. Although they weren't very close, she was the only friend Sagiko had. Tammy often seemed more vulnerable. She wanted so desperately to be accepted and liked by the others – Sagiko had accepted that she never would be – but now she seemed more tense than normal. Her voice was unusually high-pitched and she seemed over-excited. She jumped at the slightest movement, her eyes never still, looking rapidly around her like a frightened animal. Her face was strained and pale and Sagiko's concern grew as the day wore on.

Normally Sagiko thought of the journey home regretfully, but today she was almost relieved when the final bell rang. She gathered her books together as

Tammy chatted to Charlotte, obviously hoping for an invitation to come back home with her. But Charlotte listened to Tammy with a faintly bored expression before linking arms with her friends and heading towards the platform where the MechBirds landed. Tammy drifted over to Sagiko's desk, her expression miserable.

Sagiko tried to think of something to console her. 'You did really well today,' she said. 'If you keep doing this well, you'll score better than Charlotte, even if she is Wired.'

Tammy smiled the same secretive smile. 'There's Wired and there's Wired,' she said enigmatically.

'What do you mean?' Sagiko asked, frowning.

Tammy glanced around the classroom and then said in a lowered voice: 'Stop by the Island with me on the way back and I'll show you.'

The tubes were full of people when they left the school. At first the hurrying crowds were made up of Corptowners, carrying portaBrains and datacubes. But, as they reached the edge of the arcologies, where the walls began to be covered in spray paint, the majority of the passers-by were Tubetowners. A CityCrawler was drawing up outside the exit from Tube7–82 as the girls came out into the grey sunlight. Climbing aboard they showed their city passes and went to sit near the back.

The stop for the Island was halfway to the

CityWarren and Sagiko checked her watch before saying, 'I can't stay for long; I have to get back in time to make supper for Delphi.'

'Can't your mother look after herself for a change?' Tammy complained.

'She works all day,' Sagiko said levelly. 'It's only fair that I help out.'

Tammy shrugged, uninterested. Her own parents were so proud of her scholarship to a special school that they didn't expect her to help out with her brothers and sisters, since her 'study time' was so important. Only Sagiko knew how little time Tammy spent studying. At least she had thought she knew: Tammy's test results seemed to have proved her wrong.

The Island was at the edge of Tubetown. Run by a collective of Tubetowners instead of a corporation, it offered a selection of entertainments which, while not as sophisticated as the corporate entertainment centres, were cheap and fun. When Delphi had managed to save some money she would take Sagiko to an open-air concert in the Island auditorium or buy her something from the market. Tammy went there almost every day after school. When the Crawler drew up to the Island stop, almost half the passengers got off. Sagiko and Tammy went with them and were immediately swallowed up by the swirling crowds. Neon lights flashed everywhere, music blasted from all directions and market traders haggled loudly with customers. Tammy grabbed Sagiko's hand and dragged her through the crowds, heading for the virtual reality arcade. Sagiko allowed herself to be pulled along, wondering why Tammy had brought her here. At the entrance Tammy swerved left and headed down an alleyway that led to the parking lot at the back of the arcade. Crawlers were parked in rows across about half the lot and a stall selling soy-sticks was set up nearby.

Tammy was looking around intently; after a moment she gave Sagiko's hand another tug and said: 'Over there.'

Sagiko looked across the lot to where they were heading and saw a group of figures gliding towards them on silver-wheeled boots. The Bladers were all kids, not much older than her, and they called out when they saw Tammy.

As they came to a halt, their wheels hissing against the smooth surface of the parking lot, Tammy introduced them. 'That's Flip,' she said, pointing at a boy with dyed bright purple hair, 'and Yanchee' – a black boy with rainbow tattoos on his shaved head grinned at them – 'and this is Cherry' – a blonde girl, munching on a soy-stick, nodded at them and swallowed quickly.

'Hiya, Tam, who's your friend?'

'This is Sagiko,' Tammy told her. 'We go to school together.'

'Are you another Corptown wannabe?' Yanchee asked, grinning to show it was a joke.

'Not really.' Sagiko shook her head. 'I just go to school there.'

56

'Nice to meet you, Sagiko,' Flip said. 'Come and hang with us.'

The Bladers skated over to the other side of the lot, Tammy and Sagiko following, where they'd dumped their bags in a heap. Cherry fumbled in a huge rucksack to produce three bottles of pink lemonade, which they shared amongst the five of them. Sagiko leaned against the back wall of the arcade, listening as the others talked. The sun was shining and she liked Tammy's friends. She wondered why Tammy bothered trying to be friends with Charlotte when the Bladers were so much nicer to her. She still didn't know why Tammy had brought her here but she was glad she'd come.

They'd been there for about ten minutes when Tammy said casually: 'Has anyone seen Uzi around lately?'

There was a brief pause before anyone replied and Sagiko caught Yanchee and Cherry exchanging a glance before Flip replied: 'Not for a couple of hours; he's probably somewhere in the arcade.'

'I'll just have a look then,' Tammy said, getting to her feet. 'I'll be back in a minute. OK, Sagiko?'

Sagiko nodded and watched as Tammy went over to the back door of the arcade. 'Who's Uzi?' she asked.

There was another strange pause before Cherry said: 'He hangs out with us sometimes.'

'Someone should warn Tammy about him,' Yanchee said quietly.

'Why does Tammy need warning?' Sagiko asked with a frown.

The others looked at each other, then Yanchee continued: 'He deals Wireless.'

'Is that a drug?' Sagiko was getting worried. She knew that some kids her age took drugs but she never had. Delphi had warned her against them, saying: 'Half of them are things everyone knows are bad for you and even when they're not supposed to be dangerous no-one really knows for certain.'

Cherry's nod confirmed her suspicions. 'It's a smart drug, it's supposed to make you more intelligent, give you better memory, things like that.'

'You know how Corpkids with rich parents have operations and stuff to make them more clever?' Flip asked. 'It's called being Wired.'

'Lots of the kids in my school have had it done,' Sagiko said.

'Well, Wireless is a drug that does the same sort of thing. They make it from the same chemicals as the surgical implants.'

'Do you think Tammy could be taking it?' Sagiko asked, remembering her friend's high marks in the test that morning and the foil packet she had seen Tammy with in the elevator.

'I don't know.' Flip shrugged. 'But if she was, she probably wouldn't talk about it.'

'If she is, someone should warn her about it,' Cherry said. 'Wireless has all sorts of side effects. First it makes you jumpy and gives you killer headaches; later it just shuts down your brain.'

'Typical smart drug,' Yanchee said with a grimace. 'Starts off making you clever, then it turns you into a vegetable.'

'But Tammy doesn't need to take Wireless,' Flip pointed out. 'She goes to that special school, isn't that right, Sagiko? Everyone knows you only go there if you're really intelligent.'

'Yeah,' Cherry agreed with relief. 'Tammy's the last person who needs to take Wireless.'

Sagiko didn't say anything but she thought about how often the CityCrawler made them late for school, how hard the tests were now and how people like Charlotte didn't even need to work for them. She remembered how desperately Tammy wanted to be like the rich Corpkids and she stared to wonder how far her friend would go to succeed.

Tammy came back after about half an hour and no-one said anything about Wireless but Sagiko sat silently thinking and it wasn't long before she said she had to be leaving.

'Catch you later,' Flip said, and the others smiled a goodbye.

'Are you coming too?' Sagiko asked Tammy.

Tammy hesitated and then nodded. 'I suppose so,' she said. 'It looks like it's going to start raining again.'

The sky was clouding over as they walked to the

Crawler stop and the day seemed darker. Sagiko waited until the CityCrawler arrived and they had grabbed seats at the back before saying quietly: 'What do you know about Wireless, Tammy?'

Tammy looked annoyed for a second and then grinned. 'You guessed then?' she asked. 'It's brilliant. I don't need to revise at all now. I'll give you one for free if you want, but you'll have to get more for yourself.'

'I don't want to take it,' Sagiko told her. 'Haven't you heard about the side effects?'

Tammy tossed her head contemptuously. 'You shouldn't listen to rumours,' she said. 'That doesn't happen to everyone.'

'But is it worth the risk?' Sagiko asked her.

'Worth the risk?' Tammy looked at her blankly, her eyes round with surprise. 'Of course it's worth the risk. If I get high enough marks at school I might get a scholarship place at college and then I'm bound to get a job with a Corp. It's all right for Charlotte; even if she wasn't Wired her parents would buy her a place at university. I can't afford that and if I don't get a college place I'll have to stay here for ever!' She wrinkled her nose as she looked through the rain-streaked windows of the CityCrawler. 'You only just passed the test today and you won't go on passing it. Wireless is the only way out of this dump for us; if we don't take the risk we haven't got a chance.'

'What about your parents?' Sagiko asked her. 'If they found out . . .'

Tammy looked pitying. 'My parents know,' she said. 'How else do you think I get the money to pay for it? They can't afford to have me Wired but this is the next best thing.'

'Why?' Sagiko frowned, trying to understand.

'My parents want me to get educated so I can get a Corptown job and help to support them and my brothers and sisters,' Tammy told her. 'This is the best way to do it.' She shook her head at Sagiko. 'There's no need to act like you're too good to try it. Sooner or later you'll have to do something.'

'I am doing something,' Sagiko said quietly. 'I'm studying.' She met Tammy's eyes seriously. 'You taking this drug is just like Charlotte being Wired. Neither of you tries to work when you can pass without it. The only difference is that Wireless will kill you. But maybe having your brain wiped is OK if you never bother to use it.'

There was a hiss as the Crawler stopped and opened its doors and Tammy stood up. 'I should have known you wouldn't listen to me,' she said coldly. 'What do you know anyway? You're just another dumb Tubetowner.'

Sagiko watched her as she jumped down onto the pavement, braving the first drops of rain as she ran for the nearest tube entrance. The Crawler doors closed again and the machine lumbered on. Five stops later Sagiko got out and headed towards the CityWarren where she lived. The room was small, smelling of dust and books, but Sagiko relaxed when she came in. Delphi wasn't back from her job as a nurse in a public clinic and Sagiko searched through the small kitchen cupboard for something to cook for supper. She was heating the instant MealMix when her mother got home. Delphi was exhausted as usual and although she thanked Sagiko for making supper she was too tired to really notice what she was eating. Afterwards she stretched out on her bed to rest while Sagiko gathered her books together.

'Did you pass today?' Delphi asked, lifting her head a little from the pillow.

'Yes, I passed,' Sagiko told her. 'But I was late again. I need to do better tomorrow.'

'I got you some more books,' Delphi said, waving at a paper-wrapped parcel. 'I told one of the doctors about my smart daughter and he sent you some of his old school books; he thought you might like them.'

Sagiko smiled. 'Thank you,' she said, already opening the package. Brushing the covers clean, she lifted them out one by one.

'Anything good?' Delphi asked, making herself more comfortable.

'They're all good,' Sagiko said, stacking them carefully on the home-made shelves. 'I'll read one once I've revised for tomorrow's test.'

She picked up a book and curled up on her bed. Tomorrow she would have to try to talk to Tammy but right now there was nothing she could do. She felt guilty for yelling at her friend on the Crawler but she couldn't help herself. All Tammy wanted was to make friends and have fun. She took Wireless because she didn't want to study late every night just to keep up with her classmates.

Sagiko was lucky in comparison. She didn't mind working late every night. For the first time she thought about why she was studying. She wasn't as desperate as Tammy to leave Tubetown and she wasn't afraid of having to get a job. But she wanted to study. If she could understand the world, Tubetown didn't have to be a trap. There would always be new discoveries and new choices. Her only limitations were how much there was to learn and how hard it was to make the right decisions.

BELONGING
by Lisa Tuttle

This was the beginning of the end of my ordinary life:

A day in spring. I was fourteen, getting home after school to find a battlegame in progress in the middle of the living room, in full, hi-res, sensurround holo, and my mother in hysterics, weeping and wailing and carrying on like she'd just lost her dearest friend.

Among the screaming, jeering crowd of life-sized yet insubstantial figures which filled the room I could barely make out my dad, trying to hold and comfort her, saying that it was never as bad as it looked, and that even the live-action stuff was enhanced with special effects. 'He might need a transfusion, but he'll be all right.'

I didn't wonder who 'he' was – one of the battlegame stars was being stretchered off the field of battle. It had to be Gray Grayson. My mum didn't fit the profile of a typical battlegame fan: she hated violence, bloodshed and danger; she was so worried about my getting hurt that she wouldn't even let me play football. In spite of this she never missed one of Gray Grayson's contests, whether it was with swords, flame-throwers, armoured tanks or no–holds–barred wrestling.

'Don't cry, my love. Think positive. We've been through this before . . .'

I felt ashamed for him. Where was his self-respect? I'd figured out a few years earlier that Gray Grayson was my real father. There was no obvious resemblance between me and the shimmering megastar with his bulging muscles, hair like shining grey fur and silver eyes, but the first time I caught sight of Gray Grayson's son Boyd on one of the paparazzi channels, it clicked: apart from the fact that he was a couple of years older than me, and had been trained for athletics since he could toddle, he could have been my identical twin.

So, naturally I had to wonder what made *him* so special, that he got to live in the lap of luxury with his real dad, famous just for being, allowed to do and be whatever he wanted, while I was forced to grow up ordinary – less than ordinary, really, since I was never even allowed to have a bike or play football or hockey in case I hurt my ickle self . . . well, it just didn't seem fair. And when I asked my mum about it, she lied. She acted shocked that I could even dream she'd ever be unfaithful to her husband (as I knew, they'd been married for five years before I was born), and she swore blind that she'd never even *met* Gray Grayson, let alone had an affair with him. She was pretty convincing, but something more compelling – call it instinct – told me that Gray Grayson was my real father, and Boyd was my brother. If it hadn't been for the video I'd seen of my birth, I'd have been sure I was adopted. But there could be no doubt she was my mother, no matter how estranged from her I felt, no matter how baffled and angry I felt at being denied my birthright.

It was them I was mad at, not Gray Grayson, but I said loudly, 'Serve him right if he does die. He must have a death wish to go on fighting at *his* age.'

Dad jabbed at the remote, and the images around us shrank and flattened against the far wall. My parents stared at me as if I were a ghost, and my mother began to wail.

'Go to your room, Jack,' said Dad.

'You disgust me,' I said. I remember closing my bedroom door, and then . . . was I conscious of a faint hissing sound? Did I feel dizzy? Did I manage to do anything else before I collapsed? I don't know. The next thing I knew, I was lying in a hospital bed.

There was a generalized ache in the lower part of my body, but try as I might I could not remember what had happened after I'd stomped out on my folks. I groped along the edge of the bed and found a button to press.

My mother came in. 'You're awake! Oh, Jack, how are you feeling?'

'What happened?'

Her eyes skittered away from mine, and she gave a little shrug which made me suspect she wasn't going to tell me the truth. 'It's not too bad. You've lost a kidney, but really you only need one; lots of people manage with just one.'

'But what happened? I can't remember anything . . .' I shifted uncomfortably and became aware that there were bandages on my legs. 'What's wrong with my legs?'

'They'll heal in no time. It was only a little skin graft.'

'Skin graft? Why? Where? Was I in an accident? Mum, what happened?'

But I could not pin her down. She rabbited on about how a bit of skin and one kidney weren't much to lose, and began to edge towards the door. 'You'll need your rest . . . I just had to see how you were, but you should get some sleep . . .'

'Shouldn't there be a doctor in to see me — or a nurse?'

She laughed uneasily. 'Jack, you've been watching too many old videos! That kind of personalized care isn't cost-effective, or necessary. The bed's monitoring all your signs — look, there's some pills for you to take! I really shouldn't be here at all; there's a video monitor

for relatives in the waiting room, but I wanted to—'
Suddenly she darted back, bent down, kissed me, and
then she was gone.

I touched my cheek, feeling where her tear had
splashed, and then, dizzy from a surge of pain, I took
the pills from the dispensary located conveniently close
to my right hand.

I stayed in hospital for a week, and saw nobody for
most of that time except my mother, who visited for
an hour every day. I was feeling much better by her
second visit, so I was really pleased that she'd thought
to bring my PC. I didn't mind not having any other
visitors: as long as I could access the Net, I would never
be bored.

I've already mentioned that I wasn't allowed to take
part in sports – workouts at the gym were about as
physical as I got. Despite the fact that competition was
always de-emphasized at my school, I had a deep-
seated need not only to excel but to *win*. Personal best
wasn't good enough; I needed to test myself against
others.

Virtual gaming supplied the answer. I tackled all sorts
of sports and combat in the safety of virtuality. On the
Net I met others like me, and we fought with flame-
throwers, light-swords, nuclear bombs – whatever the
mind of man could devise. Some of the games
were modelled on the popular battlegames of real-time
media, but there was a major difference, in that we
were risking only virtual lives, which were infinitely

renewable. We could be as sick, violent and blood-thirsty as we liked. My spaceship might explode, with me in it, but I would still appear, whole and unbloodied, at the dinner table. My reflexes were good, and I was fearless. Over time, with practice, I became practically unbeatable.

It was after I'd got really good, with a more than respectable cumulative point-average, that I discovered the connection between the high-rated battlegames and virtual gaming. All the major battlegame stars had a presence on the Net, where members of the public could challenge them. Sometimes ordinary people defeated even the most mega of battlegame megastars in virtuality. When they did, they were offered the option of taking the challenge to the next level, and meeting the battle star in the Real Life arena of his (or her) choice.

That was my ambition. One day I would do battle with Gray Grayson, and I would *win*. And when I'd won, I'd be allowed to meet him in Real Life . . .

Of course, most people who spent enough time playing in virtuality to become champions were totally unfit for any sort of Real Life physical challenge, and most of them were smart enough to know it, and bow out before it came to actual bloodshed. Occasionally, though, they were young, fit, foolish, or obsessed enough to persist. They'd have their brief moment of glory before being horribly, painfully defeated. They were *always* defeated.

I knew it would be the same for me, but I was going to challenge him anyway. Of course he would beat me in a Real Life battlegame – there was no shame in that. He was the champion, after all. But I thought I would impress him with my courage. And when we finally met face to face, in reality, he would have to acknowledge me as his son. Maybe he didn't even know of my existence! Maybe he hadn't abandoned my mother; maybe she'd dumped him to give her faltering marriage another chance. He'd be overjoyed, when he met me, to learn that he had another son. He'd invite me home to live with him and my half-brother, Boyd. I'd be rich and famous, just like him; and for the first time in my life I would be where I belonged.

That was my fantasy.

I saw a doctor only once during my hospital stay, a few hours before I was released. I guess it couldn't be left up to a bed to decide if a patient was ready to go home.

My mother still wouldn't answer my questions, so I tried asking the doctor. He gave me an odd look, and then said abruptly, 'It's not my business. It's up to your parents what they tell you.' He snapped his scanner shut. 'You're fine. Keep using the spray skin until your legs are healed. Another few months and you won't be able to tell any difference.'

I had my own ideas about what had happened. My kidney must have failed. Maybe our health insurance wasn't enough to cover such an operation. We weren't exactly poor, but everybody knew how expensive hospitals were. Maybe they'd done a deal: recovery in a private room for a week after the operation in exchange for some of my skin and blood, for the use of another patient . . .

Well, why not? What really bothered me was the secrecy. Why couldn't my parents just tell me? Why would they never tell me anything? I really hated being lied to, and I decided I wasn't going to stand for it any more. By hook or by crook I would find out the truth.

Back home, I went trawling through our home system files and discovered that there had been no deal between the hospital and my parents. All my expenses had been paid for by the Grayson Corporation, which was a major shareholder in the hospital. I wished I could get a look at the hospital's file on me, but all patients' personal records were encrypted, and I couldn't request a copy of my own details until I was eighteen.

But just seeing that name, 'Grayson', on the screen gave me a warm feeling. It was the first piece of data I'd found which confirmed that the connection I felt was real. It also proved that he knew about me, and – since he was paying my hospital bills – that he cared.

So why did my mother deny it?

I was determined: meeting Gray Grayson face to face was the only way I could solve the mystery of my existence.

★   ★   ★

It took me another six months of steady competition in virtuality, but finally Gray Grayson accepted my challenge, and I beat him, best two out of three rounds. When I was offered the chance to meet the battle-game star in actuality, for a real-time, physical battle, I agreed immediately. I knew my own limitations, and his skills, and I had decided on tanks as the weapon of choice. Tanks were great equalizers. I already knew, from virtual war-game scenarios, what the set-up inside would be, and even if Gray Grayson had more experience, I was willing to bet my youth and swift reflexes might give me an advantage.

My previous challenges to Gray Grayson had been made using the Net-name 'Giantkiller', but public battlegames required legal contracts to sort out things like broadcasting rights, fees and merchandising shares, and for this I had to provide not only my real name, but also my civic ID number.

I didn't have a civic ID number. Most people under eighteen didn't, their main purpose being (as far as I could see) to 'protect' the young from any contact with the various pleasures, drugs and information deemed OK only for grown-ups.

I ground my teeth as the question box waited on my screen, but decided that this was only an annoying blip. I dealt with it by inserting my mother's ID number. This had worked before when I'd wanted to download some restricted information.

But this time it backfired. My screen turned shocking blue and a poison-yellow message flared

NON-LEGAL ENTITY EXCLUSION

I was disconnected. The program I'd been running gave a wailing bleat and froze. They couldn't possibly have sussed me so quickly; it must mean that for some reason my *mother* was prohibited from battlegame competition – or from attempting to contact Gray Grayson . . .

I was aware of the bleep of my mother's phone in the next room, and I heard her voice, without being able to make out the words. She let out a chilling wail.

I thought at first I was dizzy because I'd stood up too quickly, but when my legs buckled I was aware of a steady hissing from the vent in the ceiling. It reminded me of something, but before I could remember what, I was out.

The next thing I knew, I was waking up in a strange bed.

It wasn't a hospital this time, and I wasn't in any pain, just very confused. The room was large, impersonal yet discreetly luxurious. I sat up and reached for the sealed bottle of mineral water on the bedside table. I was drinking it when the door opened and a well-dressed man came in.

He could have been almost anything: a successful

businessman, a lawyer, a ruthless criminal. As it turned out, he was all three.

'Where am I?'

'This house is the property of the Grayson Corporation.'

'Gray Grayson?' My heart pounded. 'When do I meet him?'

His smile was unpleasant. 'I wouldn't be in such a hurry, if I were you. This is to be your home from now on. That door over there will take you down to a lower level where there's a recreation area, a gym and a swimming pool, and also a well-stocked kitchen. If you need anything you can key your requests into the house system.' He nodded at a console in the corner. 'You won't be allowed to leave the building, but we want your stay here to be comfortable, and your requests will be met, within reason.'

'How long am I staying here?'

'For the rest of your life.'

I laughed nervously, but it was no joke. Suddenly I was scared. 'Where's my mum?'

'Mrs Platt's contract has been terminated. She was specifically prohibited from ever attempting to contact Mr Grayson directly. After that security breach she could no longer be trusted.'

I scrambled off the bed. 'But she's my mother! You can't just take me away from her because I used her ID number!'

'You young hackers think it's all a joke, but fraud is

a serious crime.' Abruptly he dropped the heavy manner and said, 'Come on, Jack, you're a big lad now; you don't need Mummy to look after you.'

'I don't need you! Where's Gray Grayson? I want to see him. You have no right to keep me here.'

'You're wrong there, Jack,' he said with a sigh. 'You're the one who has no rights.'

'Just because Gray Grayson's my father doesn't mean he runs my life.'

'He's not your father.'

'Oh, no? Then why am I here? What's the point of all this? Tell me that.'

'You're not his son, you're his clone. Genetically identical. Even your fingerprints, your retinal pattern, your blood – there's no difference between what's his and what's yours. And Gray Grayson owns his own genetic copyright. As his lawyer, I made certain of that. Which means he owns you.'

I couldn't believe what I was hearing. None of that was true. Cloning was just another means of reproduction, legal for nearly twenty years. When we got to the subject at school, two of the kids in my biology class had identified themselves as clones. Nobody fainted, nobody locked them up. There had to be tens, if not hundreds of thousands of people in this country now whose life had started in a test tube. Only a complete imbecile would imagine that made them less than human. 'Nobody can own another person. That's slavery. It's illegal.'

'It would be illegal if you were a person, but you're not. Legally, you do not exist. Your birth was never registered, and we paid your mother for services rendered – for assistance in the reproduction of spare genetic material, wholly owned by and for the sole medical use of my client. You have just as many "rights" as the blood a lot of people keep stored for use in operations or emergencies. You're just a walking sack of spare parts. Your life is a temporary loan from the copyright holder.'

For a few seconds I was frozen with horror. Now I knew what had happened to my kidney, and to the skin on my thighs. 'That can't be right!'

'Well, that's what I'd say if it ever came to a court of law . . . I wasn't trained to plead guilty and give up. And it makes Gray feel better if he can believe you're a sort of soulless extension of himself, and not a real person like that clone he calls his son. That's why I've been careful to keep you away from him. Out of sight, out of mind. As long as nobody knows of your existence, we're safe.'

'My – my mother knows. She'd tell someone. She won't let you—'

He shook his head, smiling at my foolishness. 'Your "mother", as you like to call her, already *has* let us. She was bought and paid for years ago – she belongs to the Grayson Corporation body and soul. No doubt she was fond of you, in her way, but there was never any chance she'd risk her livelihood by going to the police.'

Learning the truth about my 'mother' was devastating. My mind was shrieking at me to rush the sleazy shyster, tackle him, attempt to escape, all the things I'd have done instinctively if this was an adventure in virtuality. In reality, the best I could do was to mutter, 'I don't belong to you. You might own her, but you'll never own me.'

'Just your body, Jack,' he said cheerfully as he left (the door, I noted, was set to respond to his palm-print). 'Your mind is your own . . . although I don't think you'll be able to think your way out of this one!'

Well, there's nothing like a challenge.

After I'd had a chance to calm down a little, I became determined that I *would* think my way out. Certainly brute strength (even presuming I had it) wouldn't be enough. Like all the modern buildings I'd ever encountered, my prison was controlled by a computer system. Give me a system and enough time, and I will hack into it. A *real* prison might have been different, but I was willing to bet my prison had been designed as a guest quarters, which meant that the palm-print key could be quickly and easily changed. I didn't try anything too fancy – I just cleared all changes made to all the locks in the house, returning them to their default setting. In most private homes the default setting is the owner's genetic code, and so it proved here. Gray Grayson was the owner and, of course, what was his was mine.

I let myself out into a long, featureless hallway, and

tried to ignore the pounding of my heart, the impulse to run like mad, knowing I was far more likely to escape if I didn't look like I was trying to.

A lift at the end of the corridor took me up a level and I emerged into a large, circular hall, with doors at intervals all along the wall, and a grand staircase in the centre. A woman in uniform was polishing the banisters. She looked at me in surprise. In a panic, I snatched at the nearest door and stumbled through.

I found myself in a room face to face with Gray Grayson.

He was relaxing in a form-fitting chair, working on something in a little notebook with holographic extensions: even from across the room and in my highly charged emotional state I recognized the configurations of the maze game where I'd beaten him.

I couldn't speak.

He glanced up at me. 'Boyd! When did you get back?'

Briefly I considered pretending to be Boyd and making my escape that way, but there was another yearning in me, even more powerful than the need to get away, and that was to be recognized, to be known by Gray Grayson for who I really was. Even if it was self-destructive, I had to confront him. 'I'm not Boyd,' I said. 'I'm Jack.'

He looked bemused. 'Aren't you a little old to be playing those kind of—' Then his eyes narrowed. 'Boyd?'

I shook my head.

He got up, slowly and cautiously as a big cat, steely eyes raking my features. 'No, you're not . . . Boyd is older, and he has a little scar below his mouth from the time he took a header off his bike . . . but who . . . how . . . you're mine, aren't you?'

My stomach clenched, but I didn't flinch, didn't run away. This was the moment I'd dreamed of, but now that I knew he wasn't my father, the reality was so horribly different, I hardly knew what to say. In spite of myself, my head was nodding. Yes, I was his. 'No,' I blurted. 'Nobody owns me – I'm my own person, even if I was cloned from you, that doesn't make me part of you – I'm still *me*.'

'Of course you are, son, of course you are . . .' He shook his head as if trying to clear it, as if he'd taken a punch. 'You're Boyd's younger twin . . . you're not me any more than he is. I found that out before he was a year old. I thought he'd be me reborn, thought we'd feel exactly the same all the time – but we didn't. Actually, I thought it would be kind of creepy, having a double, but it's not like that. He was a new baby, a new person entirely . . . he was my son.'

'I'm your son, too.'

His face crumpled – for a second I could see beneath the enhancements, the cosmetic surgery, the additional years to my very own familiar face. 'But I don't want – I don't need another son . . .' Then a cold, angry mask took over, his fighting face: 'This is a trick, isn't it? Some sort of scam. Who's your mother?'

'I'll take care of it, Gray,' said a voice from behind me, and the lawyer's hand fell heavily on my shoulder.

More horrible than that was the look of relief on my clone-father's face as he said, 'Thanks, Oz. Make sure he doesn't get back in to bother me, would you? I really don't need this kind of disruption just now. I have a challenge to prepare for. I have to beef up my virtual skills, or I'll be a laughing-stock. This maze is a killer.'

'Not for Giantkiller,' I blurted.

The lawyer was trying to pull me away, but he stopped at a gesture from his boss.

'What do you know about that?'

'Everything. I *am* Giantkiller.'

'You? You're the one who beat me, two out of three?'

'And you know why? So I could get a chance to meet you, face to face. Because I thought you were my father, and you'd be proud of me. Boy, was I dumb. I didn't realize you only wanted me to exist so you could use me – I'm fine if you need a skin-graft or a blood transfusion or even an organ-transplant, but if I want something from *you*, even just a little recognition, well, forget it.'

Gray Grayson's mouth was hanging open, and he'd gone a sickly colour. He didn't take his eyes from my face, but when he spoke, it was to his lawyer. 'Oz, is it true? Is he my . . . ?'

'Insurance, yes,' said the lawyer harshly.

'I have his kidney? But, I thought you'd bought it from a donor . . .'

'We bought the donor. Gray, for once, can you be the hard man everybody thinks you are? It's a tough old world. Everybody looks out for number one. Just leave it to me. He won't bother you again, I promise.'

'No.' Gray shook his head ponderously. 'I stopped believing that "looking out for number one" was top priority once I became a dad. I'll never forget the first time Boyd hurt himself – he burnt his little finger, grabbing at the pretty candle flame. I felt terrible! I'd have done anything to make it better, I'd've cut my own hand off if it would have helped . . . No, I stopped being the most important person in the universe a long time ago. I'm not saying I feel a special responsibility for, er, this lad here – after all, I never asked for another clone; you went behind my back to create him – but he's a person, he has rights, and –' he looked at me, and then away again quickly – 'I can't help seeing how much like Boyd he is; he is our flesh and blood.'

'Gray, be realistic,' said the lawyer. 'You're not thinking straight. Everybody at your income level, especially in the high-risk professions, has a clone tucked away somewhere for health insurance. Are you really prepared to pull the plug on the whole system? We let him go, he goes to the media, word gets out to the general public, and *bang* – lotta people get arrested, including you and me.'

'I won't tell anyone,' I said quickly, not expecting to be believed.

But Gray looked at me and he nodded. 'He won't tell anyone, because he's going to have a good life here with me and Boyd, and he won't want to see me locked up, will you, son?'

'Just what you need, another son,' said the lawyer sourly.

Gray laughed. 'No, I don't need another son. And I don't need major health insurance – not at this stage of my career. It's time for me to start moving aside for younger blood. I need to take a different direction – into the virtual games. For that, I need a personal trainer. Somebody who's really good – good enough to beat me.' He clapped both hands on my shoulders, and I felt a surge of connection, like electricity between us. 'What do you say, son? Think you could teach your old man a few tips on the computer?'

It seemed like the happy ending I'd always longed for. I had the father I'd dreamed of, and a life of luxury, although not fame. It didn't bother me that I was rarely seen in public, and then I was mis-identified as Boyd. I agreed with Gray that privacy was better, and I had everything I wanted at home. I spent long hours in virtuality, honing my skills and Gray's. I still didn't have a citizen's ID number, but that didn't matter, with Gray Grayson's password at my disposal, and although Gray never got around to formally adopting me, I figured these were technicalities to be dealt with later.

I only knew otherwise the morning I woke up in a hospital bed to find my left leg missing.

Boyd had been in a skiing accident and had broken his left leg in a particularly nasty way. The bone was shattered. Even with bone-grafts and the attentions of the most skilled of surgeons it might not heal properly; even if it healed, it wouldn't be as good as new – nothing like as good as the perfect transplant he could get from me.

Gray wept at my bedside, horribly sorry for my discomfort. Yet that's all he thinks it is; he expects me to understand, and accept, that Boyd's physical existence is more important than my own. He pointed out that a smashed leg would have finished Boyd's career as a sportsman, whereas with a prosthetic or without, with one leg or two or none, my life will continue much as before. You don't need real legs in virtuality.

Yet it's not just a technicality that I didn't hear this argument *before* my leg was amputated. I was given no choice. And my freedom to roam the Net is hardly complete. My password doesn't operate everywhere. I can't reach the media.

But there are ways of smuggling information out in code. I can't control where this message will end up when it re-emerges as text, and I don't know who will read it, or when. It will appear to be part of something else. It may be embedded in the instructions for some new piece of equipment, or a game; it may be printed inside a book, looking at first glance like just another chapter, just another story . . .

This is my cry for help. Please, whoever you are, wherever you read this, take action. All over the world, hidden away in the fortress-homes of the very rich, in private hospitals, or growing up unaware in ordinary homes, are people who are not allowed their own lives, people created for the use of others, treated like personal belongings. Investigate! Tell everyone you know, until it can't be denied as mere rumour. Spread the truth and set us free.

RANK
by Lesley Howarth

'Take it or leave it,' Parky had said, when Japeth turned up on the bus rank. 'Make up your mind, sonny Jim. Plenty of other eight-year-olds. No shortage of bus monkeys.'

Japeth had taken the job gratefully. As an underage Greeter on the public transport system – Buslink mainly – he'd have no security, of course. But since the Children's Right to Work Act of 2020, he was sure of apprentice status. So Japeth had put his head down and got on with serving coffees and meeting and greeting on the luxury commuter-line buses, and sleeping on them at night. A bus monkey had no other home, and Japeth was a bus monkey now. He'd worked the Town & Country Line – colours maroon and white – in his maroon and white uniform for about three months, when Sonny Jim joined him on the Rank. Sonny Jim was what Parky had called him. He had no other name.

Sonny Jim never spoke unless he had to. 'Night, then,' he'd say, after hours.

'Things OK today?' Japeth would ask him, but usually Sonny Jim would just shrug and bed down for the night in the crash bus.

The crash bus was supposed to provide sleeping accommodation, but most Greeters slept on their own buses, since the crash bus stank of SHED. Japeth would watch Sonny Jim slope off under the halogen security lights to catch what sleep he could. He wouldn't sleep with the other boys on the full-length reclining bus seats; instead, he'd curl up in the Greeter's cubicle, beside a coffee trolley. If he was lonely, he never showed it. Sonny Jim didn't let it get to him the way it got to some people – one reason they partied on SHED to forget the coldness of life on the rank. Everyone stuck together, of course. But it wasn't the same as family.

Japeth dimly remembered family life, before he'd left home to earn a living. His mum and dad had been absent most of the time, earning a living themselves. Japeth didn't blame them. It was every man for himself. Sometimes Japeth yearned for his mother to come. Other times he felt a burst of affection for his fellow Greeters – Redmond, Wolfie, even Parky, the depot manager. They were all the family he had.

It wasn't such a bad job, especially if you were small.

Japeth was very small. He looked about six, not eight. Regular passengers – ladies – told him he looked cute in his uniform and always tipped him well. 'Cute' was a word Japeth hated, but he had to admit that his Town & Country Line uniform was tasteful by comparison with the others – Imperial Line Greeters wore red and silver; Corinthians, blue and white; Balment Line, black and orange; Holden Line, green and gold. Most people rode the bus lines to work, since the roads were pretty dangerous. Highwaymen were common; concrete blocks dropped from footbridges onto the few passing cars that chanced the roads, not very unusual at all. To be on the roads was to stand out; to be on a bus was to be pampered. That was the company ad line, at least: 'Pampered to Death – Travel Buslink'.

Bus monkeys weren't pampered to death. Instead they got dragged to death by drivers who couldn't see them. Only weeks before Japeth donned his uniform, a bus monkey had been gripped by the doors of his own bus and dragged two stops by the arm. At eight, he'd been pretty expendable. Parky hadn't even filed a report.

Until he was older, Japeth knew, he was expendable, too. But Japeth was in no hurry to turn official. The minute he turned thirteen and Parky had to insure him properly and take him on as a Greeter, he'd sack him, Japeth knew, and take on another eight-year-old. It wasn't the way it was meant to be, but it was the way it always turned out. Japeth would have to find

88

other work then, so would Sonny Jim, and they wouldn't be alone. The Bus Rank Media Max news screens were full of doom and gloom. TWO MILLION CHILDREN UNEMPLOYED – LATEST GOVERNMENT FIGURES.

Sonny Jim worked the Holden Line, and his colours were green and gold. His uniform blazed with buttons, and tassels which swung when he moved. Jim and Japeth looked after one another. They traded routes and uniforms occasionally, and no-one noticed the trade. It meant they could move around more easily, and moving around more easily was one of the perks of the job. Since driving was illegal before the age of twenty-five – recently upped from twenty-three – this was the reason Japeth and Jim worked Public Transport in the first place. As Japeth complained to Redmond, you could work, but you couldn't drive around – what was *that* about?

Nights brought Greeters from many different lines together on the Rank under the halogen security lights that made it impossible to sleep unless you slipped on the company mask with which most Greeters were supplied. Japeth's was bottle-green velvet and covered both his eyes and his ears, so that he could shut out noise as well as the security lights. Redmond's Balment Line livery guaranteed him a bright orange mask, which had been stripped away from him so many times and flung over the walls of nearby gardens by a bunch of Corinthians who had it in for Redmond, that he'd had a Last Issue Warning and would be buying his own from now on.

Inside the buses the liveries lay down with one another – pearly-white and turquoise Corinthians with green and gold Holdens; black and orange Balment Line monkeys with silver-tasselled city-centre Imperials. Reclining three decks of seat stations, they lolled and played *Dollygun* or the computer game of the moment on the seat terminals and gambled and talked and chewed SHED while the internal music system circled trance CDs in a perpetual loop in the background, so that each bus blazed and boomed far into the night. It was during nights on the Rank that you could find out anything you wanted, from disabling smart houses on protected estates, to hacking into home order groceries through Parky's depot terminal. You could hack in through seat terminals, too, if you could disable the ever-changing company security codes, new line passwords being one of the hottest properties traded by night on the Rank. Armed with the weekly line codes, you could hack into anything you wanted.

Ordering binge foods and booze was the least of your worries, but getting them delivered meant having a home address. No-one on the Rank had had a home address in years. Redmond used No. 86 Finlay Park Crescent, completely randomly, as his home address, because it lay on the Balment Line route. Requesting early morning delivery, he would nip out

and pick up his order soon after it was delivered, charging it all to company accounts, courtesy of seat terminal 006, service number 3040, or whatever service he used. There was a limit to how long he could get away with doing it. But Redmond ordered from different terminals with different line codes every week, and was prepared to push it indefinitely.

'He won't write it off for ever,' Japeth warned. 'Parky knows you do it.'

'He knows *someone* does it, so what?' Redmond shrugged. 'It's a game,' he said, 'isn't it?'

Everything was a game to Redmond. I don't really know you at all, Japeth thought. I don't know anyone, really. Everyone does what they can. But no-one cares that much, or if they do, they chew SHED, and then they don't. And the buses run on and on, taking people to and from work – the ones who don't network at home. And the roads get emptier and emptier, except for brash new bus lines, because no-one goes *out* any more; and the toll roads charge more and more, to make ends meet. Still Japeth knew he would ride the buses as long as he could. The buses are all I know now, he thought. And the only home for *me*. Once there was something else, he thought; and sometimes his heart ached quite badly.

One day he'd say goodbye and move on, when he'd sniffed a good lead on the Rank. You could sniff out anything on the Rank by night. Even the best place to die.

'The cemetery,' Wolfie said.

'What?' Redmond gathered his brows.

'If you're going to snuff it, you may as well lay down at the cemetery,' Wolfie repeated. 'It's obvious. Saves transport time. Streamlines services all round.'

Redmond frowned again, his scalp with its bleached-in peace/SHED symbol creeping forward over his skull. 'I'm going to snuff it on Parky's desk,' he grunted. 'He'll know I never slept nights, then, because he never issued more masks.'

'Why do drivers shave and wear deodorant?' a big lad named Amis rapped out.

'They don't, do they?' Japeth raised his eyebrows.

Everyone laughed. Drivers were pigs, no breeze.

'Because they're hairy and they smell?' Redmond tried.

'You heard it before.'

'No, I smelt drivers, you mean.'

The drivers clocked in at seven, and weren't released from their security-sealed cabs until the digitally programmed seals registered the end of their shift. Inside their cabs they had everything they needed for a full seven-hour shift. But isolation made them cranky. Town & Country Line drivers weren't as bad as Imperials, who drove the city centre. Drivers were pretty fearsome. They had to be, these days. Japeth's current driver was an exception. He liked Japeth because Japeth reminded him of his son Edgcumbe, who'd recently left home.

'You miss him, I 'spect,' Japeth said.

'He's only seven.' Edgcumbe's father sighed. 'I know he's got his own life to lead, and I know they've got to leave home sometime and go out and earn their own living, but *seven* seems so young these days –'

'Same as me,' Japeth said, 'when I left home.'

Since the age of seven – before the age of seven – Japeth had slept over at friends' houses. Lots of people did, as hanging out turned into sleepovers, and sleepovers turned into moving from house to house in a group that varied but always had at its core a knot of the same faces. Japeth had hung with the crowd until he was seven, in various people's basements – basements he could hardly remember now, except they'd all smelt the same; then he'd struck out on his own. At seven and a half he'd worked the trains. At eight he'd moved on to the Rank. Most people left home by ten. You needed your independence.

Everyone hung out together. Nothing outrageous in that, though Media Max deplored current trends. There was always something on the overhead Media Max news screens about youngsters burning down houses or rubbishing malls.

EWS UPDATE 10 MAY 2032 ★ NEWS UPDATE 10 MAY LAKER MALL SCENE OF FIRE DAMAGE AS KIDS TORCH HOME OF FRIEND

So sometimes they burned down houses, usually accidentally, usually while twisted on SHED – every time it happened, everyone under sixteen was labelled a crim. But no-one could prosecute minors. Instead, they put them to work. All Japeth's friends worked, even if it was only hustling. They spent what they earned on trim – clothes – junk food, SHED and software. No-one had ever got a car yet. No-one had reached twenty-five. The rumour was, some kids made it. Some kids graduated through apprenticeships to run the company or something, and took on monkeys themselves. It wasn't all gloom and doom. Maybe young Edgcumbe had his foot on the first rung of the ladder right now. His father liked to think so, as he swung back up to his cab.

'*Move out!*' Parky roared, appearing with terrible swiftness on the Rank. 'Service lines Holden and Balment! Get your fingers out!'

Edgcumbe's father started his engine and the three-deck maroon and white Luxury Service Topper moved smoothly away on the underpass, the first of many that morning, letting out nothing but clean little farts as its engine burnt diesel substitute. It was a fresh-looking morning. As they swung out on Town & Country Route 68801, the top deck gave great views over factories, fields and the waiting lines of office workers beyond Rame Mills motorway exchange. Japeth felt thrilled and liberated, the way he always did when they rode out together on a new morning and with freshly showered commuters. He turned up the air-conditioning.

They swung past Finlay Park, morning mist rising from its fountains. They flashed past Finlay Park Crescent, Japeth grinning as he glimpsed Redmond scurrying back to his orange and black-flashed Balment Line bus with the hamper of home order goodies he'd picked up outside No. 86. He pictured the meringues and gâteaux, Squeeza-pizza, Bellypoppers, éclairs, Space Noodles, pot-crunch yoghurts and mega-size chocolate Star Bars likely to be inside it. Gob-fest tonight, he thought, picturing the scramble for the Dr Frankie's Horror Jelly Shapes plus the tubs of Dippin' Dots Ice Cream – 'The Ice Cream of the Future' – that Redmond usually ordered. Redmond had *taste* in a binge-hamper. He usually hit it just right.

'THIS STOP RAME MILLS EXCHANGE,' announced BusCom as the bus pulled up and exhaled its doors open with a hiss. Priming his top-deck coffee trolley as the first yawning commuters filed up and filled the plum seats, 'Coffee, sir?' Japeth said.

'Pass us a chocolate muffin, Redders,' big boy Wolfram howled.

Redmond chucked a muffin. Thrown from hand to hand, it finally reached Wolfie via a knot of Corinthians closely involved with Squeeza-pizza in the ground-floor back seat of the Balment Line bus. They'd waited long enough for it. Now they were going to enjoy it. All the liveries had gathered together on the binge bus as the night advanced and Parky's hour of departure

approached at last. At ten past ten exactly, Redmond
had broken open his home order hamper and distrib-
uted the cream of the food inside to his mates, and the
mates of his mates. Then the rest was up for grabs.
Redmond's hamper already lay gutted on the floor,
only the deeply unpopular fig rolls and a bottle of
accidentally ordered sugar-free lemonade remaining.

The halogen lights faltered for an instant. Across the
Rank outside the buses brooded like blocks of flats
flashed in every shade of green. *Every* colour outside
looked green under the security lights. Cameras looked
archly down from the corner of every bus bay, and
additional cameras gazed from Parky's office. In the
maintenance garages behind the Rank the wind
battered and banged something around. Somewhere a
metal door rolled back with a rumble like the sound of
thunder.

'What's that?' Japeth paused with his mini-roll half-
eaten.

They listened.

'Nothing.' Redmond shrugged. 'Anyone want this
Star Bar?'

Sonny Jim shook his head.

Abruptly the bus doors hissed open and Parky
appeared, so suddenly that Redmond only had time to
flip closed his hamper and sit on it looking flustered,
and that was it.

'So.' Parky considered the scene. 'Richard
Redmond, I want you.'

'Why?' Redmond flushed.

'I told you to stop by my office today.'

'I'm sorry, I had to get finished—'

'In my office. Now.'

'Why can't you see him here?' Wolfie asked.

'See him here,' howled the Rank pack. '*See him here, why don't you!*'

Parky cleared his throat. 'If that's the way you want it. Redmond, you're fired.'

'What?'

'You know why. You must think I'm stupid. What's that you're sitting on?'

'Weekly groceries, what else?'

'And the rest.' Parky whipped out a printout. 'SuperMart home order deliveries service, receipts numbered 00597 to 00625 for special order hampers, *all charged to company accounts.* You're lucky you're under age, monkey boy, or we'd prosecute you so hard you wouldn't know what hit you. As it is —' Parky seized Redmond by his Balment Line mandarin collar '— as it is, my job's on the line, you devious little . . .' Parky was lifting Redmond up by his jacket, the orange braid trim at his collar biting seriously now into Redmond's neck as Parky ground the words into his face. 'Eat off the company, will you, you devious — little—'

'Stop that.' Sonny Jim got up. He looked as pale as Japeth had ever seen him. 'Stop that. You can't prove a thing.'

Parky's jaw dropped. 'What's this printout? Scotch mist?'

'That doesn't prove who ordered the stuff. It just proves stuff's been ordered.'

'Leave it, Jim,' Japeth appealed, a thrill of apprehension running through him.

'Who ordered it then, Clever Dick?'

'It was me,' Jim said. 'I ordered it. Then I gave it away. You all had a bite of it – didn't you?' Jim swept them all with a scornful look, and the Rank fell suddenly quiet. 'You all had a bite of that cake – you should *all* be sacked – *shouldn't you?*'

The tic of the overhead security lights set off the ring of faces crowding the bus and the stairway, some breezy with fibs, some sharply framed in new trim, some shapeless and bleary on SHED, all of them part of it now, whatever it was, the new, hard feeling against Parky; the feeling that brought them together, a feeling they'd hardly ever had before, a feeling they hardly knew.

Parky shifted uncomfortably. 'Look. I—'

'The company owes us,' Jim said quietly. 'You underpay us, anyway.'

Parky narrowed his eyes. 'What-did-you-say?'

'I'm saying I did it.'

'I'm firing you now, Sonny Jim.'

'Jim goes, we all go.' Japeth's heart hammered.

'That's right.' Boy Wolfram shouldered his way down the aisle. He searched for words which wouldn't come. He squared his Holden Line shoulders.

Then, 'One for all, mate,' he said. 'And all for one, you know?'

The bus monkeys' strike lasted six days and nights. It even made Media Max news:

WS UPDATE 27 MAY 2032 ★ NEWS UPDATE 27 MAY 2032
TAKE ACTION ON PAY AND CONDITIONS ★ GREETERS

No-one said it would be easy, especially not Sonny Jim. By the third morning they were living off over-dates sandwich bar handouts and drinking from garage taps. They were hungry and thirsty and bored and tired of picketing the Rank, especially since Parky had drafted in blacklegs – Greeters prepared to work – from regional lines far to the north, so that the buses pulled in and out as usual manned by unfamiliar uniforms blazed in yellow, purple, brown and bars of barbaric crimson. The strikers watched despairingly. Without the drivers, they couldn't hold out. And drivers cared for no-one but themselves.

By the fifth night they were cold and miserable and worn down, and could hardly remember why they were there. Lock-out meant sleeping on benches, while overhead the garages dripped. More than twenty crestfallen Greeters shared the shelter in a welter of many-coloured coats. The rest wilted wearily in bus bays, or tried to nod off uncomfortably on the steps of secure vehicles. But every night, around ten o'clock, something happened. Tonight was no exception.

'Here she comes,' Redmond whispered.

'Who?' Japeth looked up through the rain.

'Casserole woman, who else?'

'Oh, her.' Japeth shrugged. 'So what?'

Nevertheless he watched closely as a woman carrying a pot of something-or-other took sudden shape out of the shadows. The security lights doused her in a green pall as she crossed in front of the shuttered sandwich bar, so that it was impossible to tell what colour she was really wearing, or even how old she was. Setting her pot on a concrete plinth bordering the Rank, she gave them a significant look.

'She always puts it there.' Redmond got up as the woman turned to go, stood a moment, waiting, then left the way she'd come. 'Let's see what we got tonight.'

Some kind of lamb hot pot, Japeth concluded, savouring the smell as he lifted the lid of the casserole. Hot and fragrant and filling, it drew sodden Greeters like gnats.

'Su-*per*ior.' Wolfie downed lumps of carrot and potato, huffing them cool in his mouth. 'Who's the mystery cook?'

'How do I know?' Japeth snapped. But all the same, he *did* know.

Japeth went back to work next day. So did all the others. Jim got sacked anyway. Redmond went dolefully to Parky and turned himself in and appealed. But

Parky wasn't having any. As far as Parky was concerned he'd sacked a kid for stealing, and that was that. He'd sack boy Wolfram next, whenever he got the chance.

So Jim got sacked for stealing, and that was that. Japeth tried to help him but nothing that Japeth could do could help Sonny Jim.

'Packers wanted at SuperMart,' he told Jim cheerily, after hours. 'Crash-mats provided, plus staff canteen. I'll call it up, if you want.' Flipping on the nearest seat terminal, Japeth called up job vacancies, but Sonny Jim *didn't* want.

'Leave me alone, can't you?'

'Why did you say it was you?'

'What?'

'You lost your job for nothing.'

'As hard as it is for me,' Jim said, 'what would *Redmond* have done?'

Jim had a point. Redmond was weak and hypertensive. He wouldn't have lasted a month unemployed. Without SHED, he couldn't work. Without work, he couldn't buy SHED. Probably he'd have been found on the motorway, kicked along by the few passing cars, or hanging under a bridge like a bell.

So the days went by and the strike broke, and the *memory* of the strike broke as well. That feeling that had made them stand together – what was it? – disappeared so completely, no-one could even recall it. What had it felt like, anyway, to say 'All for one' to Parky? The bus monkeys checked their tea trolleys and cleaned their buses, chewed SHED by night and played *Dollygun* and fought under the halogen lights, and Parky recorded it all on security video and smiled as he chewed down his fingernails and axed Sonny Jim on computer:

INTEGRATED PUBLIC TRANSPORT SYSTEMS
TOWN & COUNTRY BUSLINK
SUBDIVISION: PERSONNEL
POSITION: APPRENTICE GREETER
LINE: HOLDEN
NAME: 'SONNY JIM'. NO OTHER NAME
KNOWN.
STATUS: POSITION TERMINATED TWENTIETH
MAY TWENTY THIRTY-TWO.
REPORT: NOTICE GIVEN 20/05/2032. SUBJECT
CAUGHT HACKING COMPANY FILES ON
COMPUTER, APPROPRIATING GOODS UNDER
COMPANY NAME AND INCITING OTHERS AS
ACCESSORY TO CRIME. FILE FORWARDED TO
LEGAL DIVISION. UNDER-AGE SUBJECT. NO
PROSECUTION POSSIBLE UNDER CURRENT
COMPANY LEGISLATION.

Parky eyed his security screens. One of them featured Redmond, rocking dismally in a corner. The Redmond boy would be useful, now that he was under the Fear. Parky's SHED dealers would find him pretty dependent, now that he'd had a whisper – a thrill – of actually losing his job.

Parky reached for his tea and checked another screen. He frowned as the security cameras panned over Jim, lying asleep on a bench. He'd get that kid moved on. Then he'd get rid of the Japeth boy. Wolfram he'd paid off already. Unable to see why he'd copped it, the boy had ambled off swearing, underpaid and too stupid to see it. No need for knuckleheads, Parky had told him. Bright kids are two a penny.

Poor old Wolfie had had his moment of glory in standing up to Parky, the night of the strike – the night the strike was *decided*. Now Wolfie was out of work and on the scrap heap at nine. No-one but Japeth knew he supported his sister in a not-very-good flat under the Rame Mills motorway flyover. How would they manage now? Better, by far – Japeth thought that night when he asked around for Wolfie and found he'd been paid off by Parky – better by far to shut your mouth and stay on the Rank, no matter *what* it brought you.

It brought Japeth his mystery woman again. She came every night after the strike. Left a pie or a cake or a casserole. Looked at him meaningfully from a distance. He thought he knew who she was.

One day he thought he'd go and find her. So he dug out his old address. After consulting the colourful public transport bus routes map, he guessed he knew how he'd get there. That night Japeth hopped buses and rode out to Gleaners Way on the pearl-bright Corinthian Line.

He knocked on the old front door. She'd be in, if

her hours were the same – the same as he remembered when he was six and got in and shouted and shouted and *shouted*, 'Mum!' and nobody – ever – was home.

'*Mum!*' he shouted, and his voice sounded strange in the house. '*Mum! I'm home! Are you there?*'

And she *was* home. Wiping her hands.

'Japeth,' she said, looking pleased. 'Japeth – won't you come in?'

'No,' Japeth said, coming in anyway. 'What I wanted to ask you was—'

'How about a milkshake? Come through, Japeth, sit down.'

Ever so gently, her voice took him in. But not for long, Japeth thought. Not for long, with her do-as-I-say undertone, and her way of not being *there*. Japeth had had his own life for as long as he could remember. What was he going to do, hand it back to *her*?

He drained his milkshake standing up. Then they fenced each other over the chairs.

'Why did you come and find me?'

'I heard about the strike. They had it on Media Max – BUS MONKEYS WON'T PLAY BALL.'

'How did you know where I was?'

'I told you, I saw you on telly. Then I asked for you on the Rank.'

'I could have managed. I don't need your food.'

'No, but I needed to bring it.'

'Why?'

'Japeth – why do you think?'

105

Japeth felt angry and trapped. 'Why can't you leave me alone?'

'How could I leave you *more* alone? I've left you alone for ever.'

The truth in this hummed in the pans on the wall. It rattled in the sink and whispered through all the ladles: *Japeth – please come home.*

His mother advanced on him. 'You don't *want* to work the buses. We could help you get a better job – don't go, Japeth, please.'

Japeth turned at the door. He looked at his mother. '*What?*'

'Nothing,' his mother said hollowly. 'Do what you want. You always do. Everyone does what they want.'

'That's good,' Japeth said. 'Isn't it?'

'I don't know – is it?'

'I think it's good,' Japeth said. He thought of Wolfram, supporting his sister in a not-very-good flat under the flyover. Doing what you like had its downside.

'But what about everyone else?' his mother insisted. 'If nobody cares for nobody, how do we all join up?'

'We don't join up. We get around. By bus.'

'What about the future?'

'More getting around. What else is there?'

'A home. Love. Children.'

'Leave it out – what for?'

'For happiness, of course.'

'Choose SHED,' said Japeth nastily, closing the door.

*   *   *

Sonny Jim turned up on Media Max shortly after that. His pale face filled the screen as cub reporter:

'As pressure for an inquiry into work and conditions on all public transport systems grows, there are questions being asked in Parliament. Apprenticeship or exploitation?' Sonny Jim leaned closer. You could see the glint in his eyes. *'I was a bus monkey. I know what conditions are like.'*

You could have knocked Parky over with a feather as the depot Media Max beamed Sonny Jim's report on child exploitation into every home and business in the land. Parky flipped. *'Turn it off! Turn that Max off now!'*

But Jim went out on twenty channels, into every company vehicle on the overhead Max, so there was nothing that Parky could do. The bus monkeys toasted Jim that night and ate a full hamper in his honour. He made it. *He actually made it.* Parky raged around outside. He knew they had a hamper. But no report was filed.

Things went on in the same way they always had. Japeth changed lines and worked the Corinthian, swapping his maroon and white uniform for pearly-white and turquoise trim. He rode his new route with a hardened heart, wondering what was the matter with him. One day he felt like crying, the next he felt quite all right. Then one day, not long after he'd started, Japeth had a new passenger.

The passenger had got on at the Exchange and sat

down beside him. Japeth recognized the woman in the canary-yellow suit from the Rank and from his visit to her home. She'd lost her swipe card, she said, so Japeth waited patiently while she found some other plastic deep in her wallet. Tired commuters pushed in behind her, swiping their payment cards through the scanner as they boarded.

'Where to?' he asked, when she handed him a travelcard at last.

'Home,' she said.

'Home?' Japeth echoed, entering her number and handing her card back.

'Where people care for each other.'

'We care on the Rank,' Japeth said.

Two stops slid by, then three. Japeth felt her eyes on him as the doors hissed open again.

'Do they really care for you? The people you meet on the Rank?'

'We look out for each other.' Japeth thought of Sonny Jim, taking the rap for Redmond.

'What about family, Japeth?'

Japeth looked blank. 'What about it?'

Japeth's mother looked helpless. 'How do we know who we are? If we don't know what family is?'

PLEASE PAY BY SWIPE CARD, PLEASE PAY BY—

'Excuse me.' Japeth hit a button.

SWIPE CARD, PLEASE—

Swiftly disabling ALARM on his BusCom control panel, Japeth leaned into his microphone: 'Can you check your swipe cards, please? Someone's card's invalid!'

The invalid card reported to Japeth. Japeth punched in a penalty point and entered the name and address. He handed the card back. 'Automatic fine notched up. Sorry about that,' he said.

'Look at me, Japeth,' his mother said. 'I *care* about you. Do they?'

Japeth swept the bus with his eyes, a bus filled with passengers he greeted every day and served with tea and coffee. They chatted and tipped him, all right. But would they notice if he wasn't there, and some other monkey filled his shoes? Would anyone care . . . Jim? But he'd never see Jim again. Jim had escaped. He'd made it.

'I get by,' he said roughly.

'Next stop Gleaners Way,' the neutral voice of BusCom announced. 'Please watch your step on dismounting.'

His mother prepared to dismount. 'Your room's waiting,' she said. 'You don't have to live like this.'

'What – I could live like you and Dad?' Japeth made a face. 'Have kids and be out on *business* for ever, so I never actually *see* them?'

'What are you saying, Japeth – you left home because of us?'

'THIS STOP GLEANERS WAY,' BusCom repeated, more firmly.

'Come home, Japeth. Please.'

109

Japeth hesitated. Now or never. The ache in his heart resurfaced. 'I have my own life.'

'Of course.'

'See more of Dad?'

'We promise.'

'Media Max in my room. My friends hang out whenever they want. Plus my own bank account.'

Japeth's mother smiled. 'Anything else?'

'Redmond comes too.'

'Redmond?'

'He could lose his job any day. Then he'd have nowhere to go.'

The bus doors hissed open on Gleaners Way Estate. The blue roads, washed with rain, reflected the orange street lights popping on one by one in the murky late afternoon. Busy satellite dishes beamed over two hundred stations into every house filled with children whose parents were out.

Japeth's mother took his hand in hers. 'Come on, there isn't much time.'

Still Japeth hesitated. 'Separate lives?'

His mother smiled and tugged him. 'Separate but connected – Japeth, come *on*.'

'What about Redmond? And Wolfie – and Wolfie's sister?'

'You want them to live at our house as well?'

'They'll pay rent – I will, too.'

'But they might not want to live with us.'

'They might not.' Japeth loved the way she'd recognized that they might not want to. 'But I want to ask them anyway.'

'Japeth, we'll miss our stop.'

'Redmond comes too?'

His mother swallowed. Then she said: 'Redmond – and Wolfie, too.'

They stepped down together off the turquoise-and-white flashed Corinthian Line bus onto the stubbled blue pavement swimming with lines. The bus pulled away again immediately, oblivious to losing its Greeter, its commuters watching open-mouthed as their diminutive bus monkey in his hero's uniform of white and blue walked smartly away with a tall woman dressed in yellow. Japeth's mother's feet lit out ahead of his, every step, in the way they had when he was smaller. In a flash Japeth remembered the peep-toe shoes, red peep-toe shoes, she'd had when he was four. His mother's flashing feet led the way to the house on Gleaners Way that Japeth knew very well, the house he'd visited resentfully not so very long ago. He let himself remember his home. Inside it was a bedroom he'd used to call his own.

'All right, Japeth?' His mother looked down at him, her eyes filled with something that made him feel warm inside. She respected him, he knew that now. In the cold world beyond Gleaners Way, how many others could say that? 'Japeth – all right?'

Japeth looked up at her wordlessly. There was so much that he wanted to say that he could never have said on the Rank. Either it was raining or there was some other reason, Japeth thought, for the water in his eyes fuzzing his vision.

READY FOR TOMORROW
by Judy Waite

Becca Dale sat on her own at the back of the class, staring out of the window and hoping the hologram of Miss Young wouldn't scan round to where she was sitting.

It was a clear day, with hardly any smog. At least that was good news. This afternoon was Outside Time – one of the few bits of freedom in a busy week – but if the atmosphere check registered high pollution they were never allowed to go. The others didn't seem to mind having to watch the latest virtual reality video instead, but to Becca the special effects never made up for the feel of the real wind in her hair, or the real sun on her skin.

'Today we're sharing some of our "Brighter Future"

designs . . .' the Miss Young hologram spoke in its husky, slightly wavering voice.

Becca turned away from the window and began nervously running her fingers along the edge of a small black box on the desk in front of her.

'. . . And we'll start with Cain Blake – Cain, could you show us what you've come up with, please?'

Cain held up a crystal pyramid for everyone to see. 'Initially I became interested in the relationship between the space inside a pyramid, and the physical, chemical and biological processes within that space. I wanted to explore the possibility that it might be the actual shape of the pyramid, rather than the embalming, which helped to preserve Egyptian kings in their mummified conditions . . .'

The eyes of Miss Young's hologram shone their approval. 'The Egyptians were, of course, masters of their time. There is a lot to be learned from the practices of such exceptional people. Please continue.'

'I've also been experimenting with cryobiology, studying the effects of keeping living cells in freezing conditions . . .'

The Miss Young hologram's head nodded, and its thin hands twisted together. 'Excellent. Excellent.'

'As long ago as the year 2000, scientists managed to resuscitate a frozen pig's heart. It was predicted then that, at some time in the future, it would be possible to deep-freeze a living human. Maybe sick people could be deep-frozen until cures were found. Maybe astronauts could be deep-frozen, then sent off to planets light years away . . .' Cain paused as the rest of the class swivelled their chairs round to face him, listening closely. Then he turned back to the Miss Young hologram. 'But today – one hundred years later – we have still not managed to achieve the full-body freezing of human beings. I decided to combine my ideas about the possible forces at work within the pyramid, and the current research into cryobiology . . .'

Becca struggled to keep up as Cain kept talking. From what she could make out, he was developing something that could bring people back to life in the future. It would be a bit like the Egyptian mummies – only these ones wouldn't crumble to dust when you touched them. These ones would jump out of their thawed-out pyramids and start asking what was for dinner.

Becca felt sick. Next to this, her own 'Robotic Pets' invention looked like something out of the Ark. She got a sudden vision of her tiny, fluffy little robots all bleeping wildly as they shoved and shuffled, struggling to go in two by two behind the great lions and giraffes and elephants. She had a feeling that, even if they did make it up the ramp, Noah would probably chuck them overboard as soon as he saw them.

'An excellent piece of work, Cain. Well done.' The Miss Young hologram's mouth twitched into something which was almost a smile. It only ever did that when it was really, really pleased. 'Now – Rebecca

Dale – what have you prepared for us today?'

Becca stood up slowly, feeling as if a zillion space bugs were playing leapfrog in her tummy. But there was no way she was going to show her project now. She wasn't going to risk everyone laughing at her, like they did the last time after her 'Flowers Can Dream' presentation. She slid the small black box containing her 'cuddly' examples under her desk, hoping the Miss Young hologram hadn't spotted it yet. 'I . . . mine's not quite finished. I'm having trouble with the wiring . . .'

'Not quite finished?' The Miss Young hologram's twist of a smile faded, and it spoke slowly, as if even the words were alien to it. 'All assignments have strict deadlines. You should know that. We can't allow anyone to deviate. Come to my laboratory after the lesson.' It gave Becca a long look of disapproval, then turned away. 'Leah Evans – maybe we could see yours . . .'

Miss Young always looked smaller in real life. She was sort of crinkly and brown, like wrapping paper someone had screwed up and thrown away. 'You do realize, Rebecca, that you have let yourself down yet again.'

Becca looked down. She hated upsetting Miss Young. She wasn't nearly as bad as her hologram made out, and she'd been really good to Becca when she first arrived.

Now, as Miss Young spoke, she sounded not just

116

disappointed, but really sad. 'The governments of the world have built us this special school for gifted young people – a chance for us to provide the highest levels of education to the most promising future scientists. We owe it to ourselves – and to the children who come after us – not to waste this opportunity.'

Becca dropped her head. 'I'm really sorry. I just . . . I don't fit in here . . .'

Miss Young sighed. 'Fifty years ago, when I was your age, there was nothing like this school in existence. I loved all the science lessons, but none of the other children was ever interested in it like I was. I became the odd one out. They laughed at me. They called me names. Sometimes I even pretended I didn't know the answers, just so I could be more like one of them . . .' Miss Young's voice seemed to catch suddenly, and she looked away, pressing a button on the digital stressometer she always kept strapped to her wrist.

Becca saw the needle swing straight into the red – warning Miss Young that her stress levels were dangerously high. Becca saw her take a tiny yellow stress-reducing tablet from the crystal sphere on her desk. It wasn't the first time Becca had seen someone use their stressometer. Some of the other children wore them too, and just lately she'd been wondering if it might be worth putting in a request for one herself.

Becca watched Miss Young put the tablet into her mouth, then went on, 'But I can't invent things like

Cain and the others. Even the words they use make my head go all whirly. I can't make out what they're talking about half the time.'

'I don't want to hear you saying things like that. You're just as capable as anybody else in this school.' Miss Young sighed. 'However, I will need to find a punishment for you, because of your failure to meet the project deadline.'

As Miss Young spoke, Becca noticed that the yellow dye from the stress–reducing tablet had stained her tongue.

Miss Young leaned towards the monitor on her desk and flicked a button. Her anxious little eyes darted along the lists of data. 'I see you've opted for Outside Time as one of your favourite recreations, so I think I'll exclude you from the Outside activities this afternoon.'

'Oh please . . .' Becca fought back the sudden sting of tears. Miss Young had strict rules about crying.

'I know it isn't easy for you.' Miss Young looked at Becca, and her voice softened, 'You weren't selected from babyhood like most of the others, but that could even be an advantage. It may give you a fresher view on things. It may help you to come up with ideas that are really different. Now, instead of going Outside, you will spend the equivalent time in your private laboratory. I want your "Brighter Future" project ready for tomorrow. Don't let me down. Otherwise, there'll be no more Outside time for the rest of the term.'

Miss Young dismissed Becca with a wave of her hand. As Becca got up to leave she saw her press the switch on the stressometer again.

Back in her laboratory, Becca got out the samples of miniature 'cuddly' robots she'd been working on — every one of the colourful, furry shapes containing tiny nervous systems made out of wires and transmitters, which were supposed to work like artificial brains. She'd got the idea from an article on the Internet about children and pets of a hundred years ago. Of course, nobody had real pets any more, but the pictures on the screen looked sweet, and the article explained how pets had given great comfort and happiness to children in the olden days, at the turn of the century.

Only it wasn't going as well as she'd planned. The article had described how real pets had been like friends — things to talk to and share deep dark secrets and fears with. All Becca's 'cuddlies' could do was whizz round in circles and fall over. She'd managed to evolve some that wriggled a bit when you held them, but even in her loneliest moments she couldn't really imagine herself being able to share anything other than frustration with these frantic bits of fluff.

Just then, she heard voices. Hurrying to the window Becca saw the rest of the pupils marching in pairs towards the Turbine-Traveller. She wondered where they were going today. It might be a trip to Madame Tussaud's latest 'Living Hologram' exhibition — or perhaps a sightseeing tour round the ruins of the Millennium Dome.

The doors of the Turbine-Traveller slid shut, there was a high hissing whine, and then it was gone, leaving just a hazy shimmer across the parking bay.

Sadly Becca went back to her desk and tried to concentrate on her project. Dipping her hand into a box of transmitters, she attached a new wiring pattern onto the brain of the fluffy white 'cuddly' she was working on. Suddenly, the 'cuddly' gave a sort of twitch and walked forward, stopping on its own at the edge of the bench. Becca put it back to where it had started from. It twitched, walked, then stopped again. And again. And again. Becca's heart raced with excitement. This was a 'cuddly' that was thinking for itself. This was a 'cuddly' that was choosing not to fall. This, Becca decided, was going to be her 'Super Cuddly'.

She turned to the computer, ready to note down the formula.

Suddenly, from out of the corner of her eye, she saw something move.

Becca turned, startled, towards the window. Something was staring in at her from Outside. Something with strange, slanted eyes and a black, hairy face. Automatically Becca flicked the switch that dimmed the glass, and sat frozen with fear. The image was gone, but she was certain the thing was still there.

Frantically she grabbed the computer mouse,

drawing the 'thing's' shape roughly onto the screen. Then she clicked on FIND. If she could discover what it was, she might be able to work out what to do next.

FELINUS – CAT: Cats were first domesticated about 2100BC by the Ancient Egyptians . . .

Becca sat back in her chair, relief flooding over her. A cat! That was all it was. She'd never seen a real one before, and in her panic she hadn't recognized it.

Cautiously she lightened the window again, and walked over.

It was still there, its huge eyes fixed on hers, its little mouth opening and shutting in a sort of silent plea. Becca knelt down, pressing her face against the glass. It was very small – thin – probably only a kitten. But it was its eyes that really held her. They were beautiful, a calm sea-green flecked with amber and gold. Becca gazed into them for a long time, and, unblinking, the kitten gazed back.

It was a strange feeling, being so close to a wild animal. Becca wondered how it had survived. It was strange that the smog hadn't got it. Either that, or the pest control squad.

Lifting her finger experimentally, Becca ran her finger down the inside of the window. Immediately the kitten raised its paw, following her finger with its own soft pink pads. She did it again. And again. And again. And each time the kitten copied her movement. Even

121

when she changed the direction. Even when she drew a squiggly pattern on the glass.

'I have to go.' Becca pulled herself away reluctantly at last. 'I've still got to get my project ready for tomorrow.'

The kitten raised its beautiful green eyes up to hers and pressed its scraggy little body against the glass, as if it was trying to push its way in.

'You're lovely.' Becca smiled. 'I'm not surprised the Egyptians domesticated your ancestors over four thousand years ago . . .'

Suddenly a memory flashed into her head. The Miss Young hologram, speaking to Cain this morning, *'The Egyptians were, of course, masters of their time. There is a lot to be learned from the practices of such exceptional people.'*

Becca hesitated. It wouldn't hurt, surely? Just for five minutes. She might even learn something from studying its behaviour. It might even help her to improve the 'Super Cuddly'.

Still keeping her eyes on the kitten, Becca pressed a button by the side of the window. The frame slid open and, with a tiny squeak, the kitten jumped in.

It walked carefully all around the laboratory, sniffing and rubbing itself along the edges of the walls and cabinets.

It fascinated Becca. The soft, silent way it moved. The clear, clever way it seemed to think. She wanted to learn everything she could about it. Swivelling her

chair back to face the computer sc
down:

> *Cats were considered sacred in Ancient* ...en
> *a cat died, some families even had their dead pet*
> *embalmed, wrapped, and laid in a special cat-shaped*
> *coffin before being buried in a cat cemetery . . .*

Becca glanced up as the kitten still crept around the
room. Suddenly it twisted and spun, running in funny,
tight little circles. 'You'll get all dizzy,' Becca laughed
as she realized what was happening. It was chasing its
own tail.

She paged down further:

> *With new civilizations there came new trade routes. It*
> *was discovered that cats could control rat populations on*
> *ships, and also fetched good prices abroad. By about*
> *1000BC cats had begun to spread around the world . . .*

Becca glanced up at a sudden rattling sound. The
kitten had discovered an old transmitter, and was
leaping and pouncing as it rolled round the floor.

She laughed again, wondering why it was that cats
weren't considered to be pests in the past. They must
have carried the same sorts of germs and diseases as they
did now, yet nobody seemed to have suffered because
of them.

Clean, affectionate and reliable, cats became one of the most popular forms of pet, and by the late twentieth century . . .

Becca glanced up again as she heard another rattle, and then screamed. The kitten had the 'Super Cuddly' between its teeth, and was tossing it playfully into the air.

'No! Please – no!' Becca dived towards the kitten. The kitten shot sideways, just out of her reach. The 'Super Cuddly' was still in its mouth. 'Oh let me have it, please. It might break, and I haven't written down the formula yet. It will take me ages to get to that stage again . . .'

The kitten backed away from her, its beautiful green eyes suddenly wide with fright. In panic it dropped the 'Super Cuddly', then shot away behind the CD ROM storage cabinets in the corner of the room.

Becca picked up the 'Super Cuddly'. It didn't look so super now. It was wet and soggy. Bits of the white fluff had come away, showing the hard, cold metal of its body in the spaces between.

Her hand shaking, Becca put it down on the work-bench. It shuffled along to the end, then fell off with an empty clatter. She tried it again. And again. And again. 'It's no good,' she whispered sadly. 'It's lost the thinking bit. The bit that made it choose to stop for itself. The wires must have got damaged . . .' Slumping

back into her chair, she put her head in her hands and cried.

She was still crying as she felt something brush against her legs.

She was still crying as she felt something soft land on her lap.

She was still crying as something light and whiskery began tickling her face.

Becca sniffed loudly, and opened her eyes. The beautiful green eyes of the kitten were staring unblinkingly back. It gazed at her for a moment longer, then curled up in her arms, and slept.

Suddenly the 'Super Cuddly', and Miss Young, and not being able to have 'Outside' time for the rest of the term, didn't seem to matter. Feeling the comfort of the kitten's little body pressed into hers, Becca felt a rich, golden happiness filling her up. The tears dried on her cheeks, and she began to whisper to the sleeping kitten, telling it all her deepest, darkest secrets and fears.

Becca sat at the front of the class.

The Miss Young hologram turned towards her. 'Today, we're looking at Rebecca Dale's "Brighter Future" project. Rebecca – are you ready?'

Becca stood up, running her fingers along the edge of a large white box on the desk in front of her. 'What I've discovered is a fresh view on things. An idea that is really different.' She lifted the lid of the box, and the kitten's black fluffy head peered out, staring round the room with its beautiful green eyes.

There was a gasp from the others as Becca lifted the kitten out gently, and held it against her, 'Now, before you decide whether this project has worked, I'm going to tell you about how it all began, and what I was trying to do . . .'

Becca paused as the other children swivelled their chairs round to face her, listening carefully. Then she turned back to the Miss Young hologram. The kitten slipped from her lap and began to creep cautiously round the room. The children stopped looking at Becca, and their eyes nervously followed the kitten instead. Then, bravely, a couple of them leaned forward and touched it. The kitten rubbed its head against their hands. From the corner of her eye, Becca saw the kitten move across to where Cain was sitting. He stiffened. With a careless grace, the kitten sprang up onto his knees.

Cain shot Becca a terrified glance. She smiled at him, and carried on talking.

By the time she had finished, the kitten was curled up tight in Cain's lap, and Cain was stroking its ears.

'An interesting topic, Rebecca.' The eyes of the Miss Young hologram seemed strangely bright. 'Come to my laboratory after the lesson. And bring the, er – the project with you.'

★　　★　　★

Miss Young's eyes were even brighter in real life. 'You put forward a well-balanced argument and explanation on what first looked to be a very questionable subject. You're coming along nicely. However . . .' She sighed. 'We are going to have to contact the pest control squad. The creature must be crawling with all sorts of bugs, and I really can't think of a scientific reason for keeping a wild animal in this school.'

'But cats are very clean. They've even got these special hooks on their tongues to help them lick off loose hair and bits of dirt. They look after themselves, and they've given people comfort and happiness for centuries . . .'

'The world has moved on. A lot of the old ways have gone for ever. It's part of the evolutionary process . . .' Miss Young pressed the button on her stressometer.

'There's another experiment I'd like to try. If it doesn't work, I'll agree with you that we should contact pest control. I only need another week.'

Miss Young took a yellow tablet from the crystal sphere and rolled it between her fingers. 'Go on.'

'In the twentieth century, as well as making wonderful pets, cats had practical, medicinal uses . . .'

'Such as?'

'It was actually proven that stroking a pet – such as a cat – could lower stress levels. Doctors even encouraged their patients to get pets – such as cats – for that very reason . . .'

Miss Young put the tablet back down again. Becca noticed that her fingers were stained yellow from the dye.

She took a deep breath and looked straight at Miss Young. 'I want to leave the kitten with you for six days. In that time you mustn't take any more tablets. Measure yourself on the stressometer at hourly intervals. Your levels should start going down. On the seventh day I'll take the kitten away again. If you record a rise after that, then you'll know . . .'

Miss Young looked from Becca to the kitten, then back to Becca again. 'Just seven days, Rebecca. For scientific purposes.'

'Thank you, Miss Young. You won't regret it, I know you won't.'

Becca stood up and handed the kitten across the table to Miss Young, then turned to go. As she reached the door, she glanced back quickly. The kitten was gazing up at Miss Young with its beautiful green eyes. Miss Young was gazing back.

Then Becca saw Miss Young's mouth twist into something which was, quite definitely, a smile.

THE MONKEY PUZZLE
by Mat Coward

We stood in front of the ape house, on a grey, harsh
day, and watched the chimpanzees watching us. I asked
my mum, 'Which one is our client?'

'*My* client, Larry,' she said. She doesn't like me
helping her out too much – reckons it interferes with
my schoolwork. Which it does.

'Your client,' I said. 'Which one?'

There were fourteen chimps. They were huddled
together in the furthest corner, as still as the dead. No
– stiller than that. As still as the scared. Only their eyes
moved . . . watching us watching them.

'I don't know,' said Mum. 'Let's ask.' She shifted her
bag up onto her shoulder, so as to free both her hands.
Everyone in my family is fluent in the sign language

known as NUS – New Universal Sign. My dad was born deaf.

I watched Mum's hands as they spelled out the message: 'My name is Ruby Potter. One of you asked to see me. Which one?'

Nothing happened for maybe half a minute, and then slowly, with fear written in every step, a chimp with a white flash of fur on his forehead made his way towards the invisible laser fence that separated his world from ours. Behind him, several of his mates covered their faces with their hands, as if they couldn't bear to watch.

When he was only an arm's length away from us, he stopped and studied our faces – first Mum's, then mine – for a few tense moments. Finally, he 'spoke'.

'I am Bobby. I'm the one you're looking for,' he signed, his hands moving rapidly. 'Please – you must get me out of here!'

My mum's a lawyer (my dad died of a terrible illness in 2052, when I was seven). Mum specializes in civil rights. If you're being oppressed by your government, my mum's the lawyer you want on your side. She's even a bit famous. Last year she took on the European Union over some American refugees that the Euros wanted to deport. Mum won the case, and got her face on the cover of a few magazines. Bobby the chimp had contacted her through a disillusioned former employee of BioFutures, his owners, who'd become an Apes' Rights activist.

The hearing was held at the New Bailey, by the Thames in Southwark, the most important courts of justice in Britain. The building had only been finished a year earlier, in 2056. It was a pretty impressive place. The outside was made of 'active glass'. It's a kind of living plastic, so it constantly gives the illusion of changing colour, morphing its shape and so on.

Because of what the judge called 'the unique circumstances', I was allowed to sit next to Bobby in the witness box during the hearing. I held his hand — or he held mine, I'm not sure which way round it was.

'You all right, Bobby?' I whispered. He could read lips as well as hands.

'OK,' he signed back. 'For now.'

Mum insisted on teaching me NUS alongside English right from when I was born, because it was Dad's native tongue. As a result, I'm about as good at NUS as any non-deaf person you'll ever meet — though Bobby, I quickly realized, was my equal.

'What is the difference between a monkey and a man?' were Mum's first words to the court. She always likes to start with a bang — 'Waking the court up, in case they've all nodded off,' she calls it.

She pointed at Bobby, and all eyes in the chamber followed her finger as she continued: 'My client, a chimpanzee named Bobby, is currently the property of a multinational medical research company called

BioFutures. Bobby's case is very simple. He says that because he can communicate meaningfully with humans, he should have the same legal rights as a human. He cannot be anyone's property, since slavery is illegal. He is not a thing, but a person.'

Bobby nodded emphatically at this point, and just about everyone in the court jumped in their seats. Being told you've got an intelligent chimp in the room is one thing – seeing it with your own eyes is another.

'Behind this simple claim, however,' Mum continued, 'lies one of the greatest scientific and moral controversies of all time. Bobby is twenty-five years old, and was born at the Animal Speech Research Center in California, where he spent his early life. However, following the break-up of the USA, Bobby was sold to BioFutures. His new owners have no interest in speech research, and so Bobby is currently used to test bio-war vaccines.' Mum picked up a sheaf of notes. 'This case is certainly one of the strangest and most important that any court of law has ever heard. I therefore offer Your Honour some background information.'

The judge nodded his approval.

'Humans have tried for centuries to teach animals to speak. The first major breakthrough came in the 1940s, when researchers realized that animals could not speak out loud, as their vocal chords are too different to those of humans, but could be taught sign language. Throughout the rest of the twentieth century researchers in America and elsewhere made progress in communicating with various apes, as well as dolphins, pigs and even parrots. But it soon became clear that Bonobo chimps, such as Bobby, made the best "talkers".'

Bobby gave her a thumbs-up sign, which caused another ripple of sensation in the courtroom.

'Bonobos tell lies, play jokes and sulk. They shake their fists when they're angry. They kiss and hold hands to show affection. By the beginning of this century we knew a great deal about the similarities between apes and humans. We knew that chimps live in complex social groups, that they use tools. That they have a natural ability to learn language – even to add up. Some captive apes became famous for their large vocabularies. Koko, a gorilla in San Francisco, knew two thousand words of English, and was taught to use the Internet. She had a pet kitten called Smoky, and she cried like any pet-owner would when Smoky was killed by a car. She even learned how to swear, Your Honour – using the word "toilet" to mean "bad".'

Bobby covered his mouth at that, and made big eyes at me. Even the judge had a bit of a chuckle.

Mum continued. 'Chimp and human DNA is 98.4 per cent identical. It is because apes are so similar to us that we use so many of them for experiments. Perhaps it is also because they are so similar to us that we are somewhat afraid of them.

'Independent expert testimony will prove beyond

doubt that Bobby now has a command of language similar to that of a human teenager. The facts are not in dispute. The only question now is: what do we do about it? For more than sixty years some philosophers have argued that apes and humans are so similar that there is no good scientific reason for the law to treat them as different species.'

Mum put her notes back on the table, and looked straight at the judge. 'It is on that basis, Your Honour, that my client demands his freedom.'

The result of that first day was that the judge ordered that Bobby should live temporarily with his lawyer, Mum, while the case continued. Bobby was thrilled: he was free from his cage, at least for now.

I have bunk-beds in my room, for when my cousins come to stay. Being a polite host, I asked Bobby which bunk he fancied.

He looked at me, looked at the beds, then he made a kind of whimpering noise in his throat.

'It's OK,' I said. 'You can have the bottom bunk if you don't like heights.'

Bobby shook his head. 'It's not that,' he signed. 'It's . . . I'm not used to making a *choice*. In the labs, they tell us what to do and we do it.'

I put my arm round his little shoulders, and told him not to worry. I was about to choose for him, but then I thought: No, pal. If you want to be treated like a person, you'd better get used to making choices.

So I said, 'Well, Bobby? Top or bottom?'

He looked up at me, the fear still on his face. But then he must have seen I was smiling, because he let out a laugh – an odd sort of noise, but definitely a laugh – and leaped up onto the top bed. 'This is mine!' he signed.

Could a chimp have the same rights as a human? I liked Bobby, right from the start. But I've got to admit, the main reason I liked him at first was that he was cute and fluffy, with that white flash on his head, and he had this funny, bow-legged walk. He was like a hairy toy, and the fact that he could talk just made him more fun to play with.

I lay there that first night, Bobby silent in the bunk bed above mine, and I tried to figure it out. If you look at an ape, you know right away it's not a member of our species. That seemed clear enough. But if you go beyond appearances – what does *human* mean?

Humans feel pain, fear, love, hunger, excitement. So do animals. Humans respond to their feelings by eating, drinking, screaming, running, mating. So do animals. Which left, as far as I could figure, lying in the silent dark that night, only one absolute difference between humans and animals: humans speak to each other.

And so did Bobby . . .

The next couple of weeks were just about the happiest I'd ever known. Think I'm exaggerating? Well, listen, it's not often you get a chance in life to make someone else really happy just by doing the things you love doing. But as Bobby and I bounced on the beds, climbed the monkey puzzle tree in the garden, and chatted away about every subject under the sun, it was wonderful to see the fear fading from Bobby's eyes, to be replaced by fun and mischief.

Within a short time Bobby and I had become real mates. I was no longer looking after him to help Mum out; I was hanging around with him because I wanted to. It wasn't that I'd forgotten he was a chimp, or anything. It was simply that – well, if you can understand what I mean, he was a chimp second, and a friend first.

Every weekday Mum, Bobby and I went to the New Bailey, and Bobby and I sat next to each other, chatting away in sign language. I couldn't really tell whether we were winning or not – legal people speak a language of their own, which is a lot harder to understand than either English or NUS – but Mum seemed mildly optimistic.

'I don't want you getting your hopes up too high, Larry,' she told me one day, about a week into the proceedings. 'I think we're doing quite well, but you've got to understand there's a lot at stake here. Not just for Bobby. Supposing they do give Bobby his freedom. That means that he's a person, not a thing. Yes? Which in turn means that he's got the right to a job, a place to live. The right to vote in elections. The right—'

'Well, why not?' I protested. 'He *is* a person!'

She sighed and put her arm around me. 'But it's not just him, is it?' she said quietly. 'Bobby's case could create what's called a precedent. That means, basically, that if Bobby has these rights – then so does every other animal who can be taught to communicate with humans. The world is unstable enough, these days. Perhaps the belief that we're superior to other animals is the only thing keeping the human race together. Powerful people stand to lose huge amounts of money if Bobby wins. All I'm saying is, we'll do our best for Bobby – but try to be strong whatever happens.'

'You mean, after all this, Bobby could still end up back in a cage?'

Mum didn't answer that. Instead she said: 'One thing that is working for us, is that you and Bobby obviously get on so well. That's having an effect on the judge and jury, I'm sure of it. Seeing your friendship with their own eyes – that's like a practical demonstration of everything we've been arguing for.'

So, all in all, things weren't looking too bad.

And then, the next day, the world fell in on my head.

It was a Sunday. Mum had taken Bobby to have some tests done with a speech expert. I'd been to visit a mate, and it was getting dark as I turned the corner into our street.

'Excuse me, Larry – could I have a word?'

A woman stepped out of the shadows. She was

smartly dressed, about my mum's age, with a kind smile. In fact, she reminded me of Mum quite a lot. 'Who are you?' I asked, but as I said it, I suddenly recognized her. 'You're with BioFutures! I've seen you in court. You're not supposed to be talking to me.'

'That's right,' she said. 'I could get into a lot of trouble with the judge for doing this. But you see, Larry, I think you have a right to know what's going on.'

I looked around. There was no-one else in sight. Still, I felt safe enough in my own street, just a minute's walk from my own front door. 'OK,' I said. 'Talk.'

The woman sighed – reminding me even more of Mum. 'There's no easy way of telling you this, Larry – but someone has to tell you. The experimental animal you have living with you—'

'Bobby,' I interrupted. 'His name's Bobby.'

'Bobby. I don't suppose anyone's explained to you exactly what sort of work BioFutures used him for?'

'Bio-weapons,' I said. 'Filthy crap designed for mass killing. Very profitable for your masters, I'm sure.'

She nodded. 'Very profitable indeed.'

I had to admit, I liked the way she spoke to me as if I was an adult, not a stupid kid.

'Especially the Peacekeepers' Sickness, Larry. That was a best-seller all around the world.'

I gasped as if she'd slapped me. It was a moment before I could speak, and when I did, my voice came hoarsely from a dry throat. 'I'm not an idiot. I know what you're trying to do. You're worried that Bobby and I are creating a good impression in court – you want to split us up with your lies!'

The woman shrugged. 'Bobby was one of the original carriers of the sickness. He was deployed in Ibiza at the same time as your father was on leave there. Ask your mother if you don't believe me.'

'Now I know you're lying,' I said. 'Mum would never have taken on the case if she'd thought Bobby was responsible for what happened to Dad.'

The kind-faced woman gave me a sad smile. 'Don't be too hard on your mother, Larry. She's an idealist – to her, ideas are always more important than people. But if you still think I'm lying, then I'll tell you where you can find the proof.'

Mum and Bobby were in the kitchen when I got home.

'Hi, love,' said Mum. 'Vegeburgers and chips, OK? Be about five minutes.'

'Hey, Larry,' Bobby signed, 'the tests went really well. We—'

I marched straight past them, up the stairs to Mum's room. I found the small, plastic box exactly where the smiling woman said it would be. I'd never seen it before, never even knew it existed. Not surprising, really: this box contained my dad's personal effects, returned to us after his death. I didn't suppose Mum had ever done more than glance at it, then stick it at

141

the bottom of an old chest and try to forget about it, and what it represented.

It contained the sort of things you'd expect. A comb, a shaving kit, a small holo of me and Mum, various personal items like letters from us to Dad, and – a photo.

'That's you, isn't it?' Back in the kitchen, I stuck the old-fashioned, 2-D photo under Bobby's nose. He backed away from it, making stupid, gibbering monkey noises. 'You lousy monkey, you killed my dad!'

I pushed him away from me in disgust, and turned on my mother. 'And you knew about this, didn't you?'

'I knew Bobby had been used in research concerning Peacekeepers' Sickness, yes,' she said. 'But listen, Larry, it's not that simple—'

'I know,' I sneered. 'Ideas are more important than people!' She started crying as I said: 'The monkey's a murderer, and you're a traitor!'

I ran out of the house, clutching the photo, and I didn't look back.

The twenty-first century was born in blood and thunder. All over the world, on every continent, there are literally dozens of wars going on right now. These are called 'mini-wars' because they involve only one or two nations, or fragments of nations, or tribes. But everybody knows that any one of those mini-wars could suddenly blow up into a full-scale holocaust that would engulf the planet.

142

By 2010 the country formerly known as Russia was a mess of feuding factions. Fifteen years later the USA went the same way; last count I heard, there were more than 150 'independent states' in North America. China is anybody's guess: in the last thirty years or so the world hasn't heard much from China (or vice versa, depending on your point of view). Some folk say it's a miracle that mankind hasn't destroyed itself yet, but in my opinion the reason we're still here isn't anything supernatural: it's all down to the peacekeepers.

I'm biased. My dad was an officer in the world's biggest army – the Global Peacekeeping Force. The GPF was set up in 2027 by some of the more stable nations – Republic of the British Isles, Southern African League, Cuba, and so on. It doesn't try to stop people fighting. That would be a hopeless task. The men and women of the GPF aren't fighters, they're more like firefighters – their job is to stop mini-wars growing into world wars, by preventing the use of nuclear, chemical and biological weapons.

Dad specialized in finding and neutralizing bio-weapons in war zones, and that kind of work is exactly as dangerous as it sounds. My dad was a hero, and I don't care who knows it. But it wasn't on the battle-fields of Florida that he died – it was while he was on leave, on a beach in Ibiza.

The Peacekeepers' Sickness killed his entire platoon: not one survivor. Over the next two years it killed a further 7,000 GPF members worldwide, plus an unknown number of civilians. Eventually a vaccine was developed, but even now dozens of peacekeepers die of the sickness every year.

It's not a pretty death. Slowly, over a period of weeks, all the soft tissue in the victim's body turns solid. There is no treatment and no cure. Ultimately, death is by suffocation.

That's how my dad died.

Thanks to my new best friend, Bobby.

What the smiling woman told me was that Bobby, and others like him, were used by terrorists to infect the GPF with the sickness. The chimps could carry the man-made disease without suffering from it themselves, and they could pass it on to humans with the slightest scratch or bite.

In Ibiza, in those days, off-duty peacekeepers would often have their photographs taken, cuddling tame chimps – a tacky tourist souvenir. The photo I'd found in Dad's box, where the smiling woman said it would be, showed Dad, looking younger than I remembered him, wearing his tourist outfit of shorts and baggy shirt, smiling into the camera while he held a cute chimp in his arms. The chimp was unmistakably Bobby, with that distinctive white flash on his forehead.

My best friend, the murderer.

I didn't sleep that night. I just wandered the streets of London, trying to imagine how Mum could have betrayed me and Dad like that. Whenever I saw cops I hid, in case they were looking for me.

In the morning I queued to get into the public gallery at the New Bailey. Looking down into the courtroom, I could see Mum and Bobby. He looked small and afraid and pathetic. She looked as if she hadn't slept for a year. *Good*: served them both right.

Just before the proceedings got under way, a court official whispered something to Mum, and she looked up into the gallery. When she saw me sitting there, her knees sagged and her eyes closed. She waved. I didn't wave back.

Mum pointed me out to Bobby. He signed up at me: 'Are you OK?'

I signed back: 'Drop dead, monkey.'

He turned away, and I saw Mum rubbing his back, the way she used to rub mine when I woke up crying after dreaming about Dad.

The sight of the two of them made me feel sick. I got up to leave – to go home, or maybe not, I hadn't decided – but just then I spotted the smiling woman sitting with the BioFutures lawyers. She gave me a big, warm smile and even blew me a kiss – and for some reason that made me feel even sicker. Confused, I sat down again.

The judge and jury were taking their seats, and the usher was calling order. Bobby, I now saw, had been watching the BioFutures woman. He began signing to me. As everyone in the courtroom got to their feet, I could only see bits of Bobby's message: '. . . sorry . . . friends . . . try to understand . . .' And then as everyone sat down again, I caught the last bit loud and clear: 'Just ask yourself – why does BioFutures want me back so badly? One chimp among thousands? Maybe we know the answer between us.'

Between us, I thought. There is no 'us'. Bobby had killed my father, why should I care what happened to him?

The day's hearing began, and it didn't take the jury long to spot that I was sitting in the public gallery, instead of next to the chimp. It was clear from their faces that they thought that was significant. Clear from the faces around the BioFutures table that *they* did, too.

Good. If I lost Mum and Bobby the case, so what? It was what they deserved.

But I couldn't help thinking that Bobby did look so alone . . . so scared . . .

And the BioFutures woman was looking up at me again, smiling, laughing with her colleagues. Laughing at me. Laughing at Bobby. Laughing at Mum.

Suddenly I heard my father's voice in my head as clear as anything. Just before he left for what turned out to be his final mission, I'd asked him if he was going to die. I'd never asked that before. I suppose I was old enough then to realize that what he did was dangerous – and that even dads could die.

He didn't lie to me. He couldn't promise he wouldn't die, he said, but he did promise to be careful.

He said he loved me, and he said something else, which echoed in my head now, sitting in the New Bailey: 'The way to survive in a dangerous situation is to know who your friends are and who your enemies are. Always trust your friends, and never trust your enemies.' It was just about the last thing he ever said to me, and now I felt that for the first time I knew exactly what he'd meant.

All that stuff about whether an ape could have the same rights as a human, and about the rights and wrongs of animal experimentation, kind of melted away. I was left with one simple fact: Bobby was my friend. As for my enemy – my *real* enemy – that was whoever had used Bobby, the slave chimp, to kill my father.

This next bit takes longer to tell than it did to happen.

I whistled, loudly. Bobby looked up at me. So did the smiling woman.

To Bobby, I signed: 'I know what we know! Tell Mum, quick – I have vital new evidence!'

The smiling woman wasn't smiling any more. She knew I was up to something, and she didn't like it. I saw her speak rapidly into a button-phone.

Bobby tugged at Mum's sleeve until he had her attention focused on his talking hands.

Just then, I felt a strong hand pressing down on my left shoulder. I turned to the left, and as I did so another hand dipped into my jacket pocket from the right. The pickpocket was gone almost before I realized what had happened. I caught just a glimpse of a tall, bald-headed man moving swiftly through the crowded public gallery. I recognized him. Last time I'd looked, he had been sitting at the BioFutures table, along with the lawyers and the smiling woman.

I whistled again. Bobby and Mum looked up. I signed as fast as I could, describing the thief. 'He's got the photo in his pocket. Stop him!'

Mum shrugged: my signing was too fast for her. Bobby repeated the message to her, slowly and clearly. She spoke urgently to the court protection officer. There was a lot of pointing, urgent whispering, then shouting, and people running in the corridors. A gunshot rang out. Uniformed police were dashing in all directions.

I looked down at the BioFutures table, and saw that the smiling woman had vanished. They caught the bald pickpocket within minutes − he'd only fired his gun once, and he'd missed with that − but they never did find out what became of the smiling woman.

'How did the smiling woman know the photo existed?' I asked Mum, much later that day, when we were home and alone at last − the three of us.

'My guess is that BioFutures burgled our house, looking for something they could use to discredit me,' said Mum. 'Instead, they found the photo, which they thought was even better.' She shuddered. I shuddered in agreement − it was a creepy thought.

Once the photo of Dad and Bobby had been officially introduced as evidence, everything changed.

On its own, the souvenir snapshot didn't prove that Bobby had infected Dad with Peacekeepers' Sickness – but along with Bobby's own testimony it certainly got people thinking. The one thing no-one could deny was that the chimp in the picture, with his unmistakable white flash, had been the property of BioFutures at the time that the picture was taken.

In other words, if Bobby had been used to infect the GPF with the sickness, it hadn't been terrorists who'd organized the attack – but good old respectable BioFutures, busy protecting their rich markets in bioweapons from those interfering busybodies, the peacekeepers.

There have been lots of arrests, and BioFutures has been closed down by the government pending a full investigation. Mum says that it'll take years to unravel completely, but that in the end a lot of rich, powerful people will be very lucky not to end up behind bars.

Good. Serves them right.

Bobby had a question. 'Why did the smiling woman tell Larry about the photo? She'd have been wiser to destroy it, surely?'

I had to laugh at that. 'Thing is, Bobby, she thought because I'm just an immature, emotional kid, I'd never be able to figure out the significance of what she told me. I'd be too busy hating you and Mum to have time to think. That's how most adults treat most children most of the time,' I added. 'You're going to have to get used to that, Bobby.'

He is, too.

Bobby lives with me and Mum now, permanently. I introduce him to people as my brother, and when they look puzzled I explain, 'He's adopted, of course.'

Next term Bobby will be starting in my class at school – the first non-human ever to go to a proper school. Now that *is* going to be fun: you see, I happen to know that only two people in our year speak fluent sign language – and that's me and my brother, Bobby.

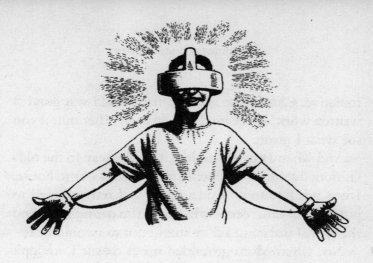

MY VIRTUAL DAD
by Nick Gifford

I still visit my virtual dad, despite what has happened between us. I don't hold all the secrets and lies against him in any way.

'Put it down to experience.' I'm sure that's what my old therapist would tell me if I gave her the chance. It all seems a lot easier to handle now, but back when I was an angry eleven-year-old things seemed very different . . .

I suppose it all really started that time when Mum grounded me for collaborating on my homework with Clifton Grainger.

'It's not "collaborating", Jim,' she said at the time. 'It's *cheating*.'

I still think that's a bit harsh: we were just using our

initiative. Clifton was good at maths and I was good at written work, so we used to help each other out, if you see what I mean.

And when I say 'grounded', I don't mean in the old-fashioned sense of not being allowed out of the house. I was still free to go out, so long as I remembered to put on the sunscreen – what with the ozone holes and the global warming I'd be stupid not to, wouldn't I?

No, when Mum grounded me it meant I couldn't go unsupervised into virtual reality.

Of course, that didn't stop me. I was always in trouble back then and I hated it when someone said I couldn't do something.

My school Behaviour Officer told me it was because my father was on the other side of the world. She said I should work it through with my therapist. Behaviour Officers always say that. They think therapy solves everything. Mum was in therapy almost all the time, back then: it didn't seem to be doing *her* much good, I always argued.

That was my trouble, I guess: I always argued. I always thought I knew the answers.

So being grounded wasn't much of a problem. I just pulled on a hat and cape to protect myself against the monsoon rain (global warming brings us all kinds of tropical weather, even in Norfolk) and trudged across the city to visit Clifton.

Clifton had a virtual reality deck that was nearly as fast as mine.

'Hi, Jim,' he said when he opened the door and saw me dripping and steaming on his doorstep. 'Grounded again?' Let's say it was a fairly regular thing . . .

A short time later we were up in his den in the attic. I pulled on his spare headset and secured the strap under my chin. I couldn't see a thing with the headset's visor down in front of my face. When I pulled on the gloves and boots I was ready to go.

'OK?' said Clifton through the headset.

There was a flash, then everything went grey. Words appeared before my eyes: READY TO GO? I nodded, and an image of a door replaced the words.

When I raised my hand I felt the surface of the door through the VR glove. I pushed and the door swung away from me. Bright sunlight bathed a street full of hurrying people. It all seemed and felt so real, yet I knew it was an illusion. The visor beamed a stream of moving pictures directly into my eyes and the sounds from the street came through speakers in the headset. The feeling of standing on a paved surface was relayed through the VR boots I was wearing.

Clifton was off through the crowd already, heading for a virtual games arcade, where he had a season ticket. Clifton and I weren't so much friends as school colleagues: we helped each other out, but that didn't mean we had to spend all our time together.

That suited me fine, that morning. 'Call my dad,' I told the headset. It was the middle of the night in Tuvalu, but I knew Dad would want to see me. He

153

always made time for me, whether he was working or asleep. It's one of the prices of having to work halfway around the world, he once told me.

'Hey, Jimbo,' he said in my ear. 'Where shall we meet?'

'Can I come and see you?' I asked.

'Sure,' he said. 'Come on over.' With that, a door appeared in a nearby wall. I went over, pushed at it and walked through.

Suddenly I was wearing frayed, knee-length shorts, and the sun was beating down on my bare shoulders. The sky was a pure, even blue, and the sea, off to my right, was dark and flat, like a deep blue sheet of glass. I was standing on sand so white it was dazzling in the bright sunlight. I wriggled my toes and I really could feel the harsh, gritty texture of the coral sand.

A big hand clapped me on the shoulder and I looked up.

Dad stood there, smiling his lopsided smile. 'Good to see you, Jim,' he said, as he always does. 'So what's been happening in Norwich, then? Is your mother keeping well?'

'Another tropical storm,' I told him. 'The monsoon season's started early this year. When are you coming home, Dad?' I hadn't meant to say that; it just slipped out.

He shrugged and we started to walk. 'It's tough on you, I know,' he said. 'It's tough on me, too. But my work's important, Jimbo. I can't just leave it.'

He waved a hand at the surroundings: the sea, the white beach, the fringe of coconut palms. 'Looks great, doesn't it?' he said. 'But in virtual reality it can look however the programmers say. This is Vaitupu, one of the smaller islands in the Tuvalu group. Or rather, this is what it looked like about a hundred years ago, before global warming.

'It's not like this any more. These islands are built up on old coral reefs, but now that the sea has risen, a lot of the islands have been flooded. Most of the coral has been killed off by the warmer water, and what's left can't grow fast enough to protect the surviving islands.'

We climbed the beach. Through the palms I could see a village: chickens, pigs and children running about between fishing boats pulled up for repairs and huts with corrugated tin roofs.

'In the real world that village has been abandoned. My team is building the island up with rock and old coral dredged from the seabed. It's a mess, but eventually the villagers will be able to return.'

'How are your corals?' I asked. Dad was a biologist. He was trying to develop genetically modified corals that would grow quickly and form a reef that would protect the rebuilt island from the violent tropical storms the warming had caused.

He grinned proudly. 'They're doing well,' he said. 'In fact—'

That was when Mum butted in. Or rather, that was when my virtual travels were interrupted by a software agent she'd hired to keep me grounded.

Everything froze. Or rather, I could still move, back in Clifton Grainger's spare VR suit, but nothing I did had any effect on what I was seeing or doing on that virtual Pacific island with my virtual dad. He just stood at my side, one foot suspended in mid-stride. Up above us, some kind of tropical seabird hung in mid-air as if it had been painted onto the sky.

A set of big, red words appeared before my eyes: CYBER-GUARDIAN OVERRIDE. Then, a few seconds later, a set of smaller words appeared underneath: YOU ARE BEING EJECTED FROM VIRTUAL REALITY. PLEASE PREPARE FOR THE REAL WORLD.

When everything had gone to grey I peeled off the gloves and boots and slid the headset up over my eyes. Clifton was still going strong, twitching and grunting as he played some virtual game in his arcade. I left quietly.

I don't know if that was when I decided to take action or if it was half an hour later, when I walked in through our back door and was confronted by Mum in her dressing gown and rollers.

I knew she was having a bad day by the green patches on her arm.

The patches contained mood-controlling drugs prescribed by her therapist: stick a patch on your arm and it released its drug steadily into your bloodstream for up to a week. I'd learned the coded language of my mother's drug patches: yellows were normal, just to keep her going. Blues kept her energy levels high, for when she had a lot of work or when she was feeling under the weather. Greens . . . greens always meant trouble.

That day she had green patches all the way from her wrist to her elbow and then probably more, but the sleeve of her robe got in the way and I couldn't see.

'It's no good, Jim,' she said in a low, angry grumble. 'It really is no good. I've spoken with your Behaviour Officer, and we've made recommendations to your therapist. You really have to learn what is acceptable behaviour and what is not. Are you listening, Jim?'

I shrugged, then grunted something when she demanded a response.

She was saying something, and I thought I'd better start listening: '. . . far too dependent on it – it can't be good for you. From now on there'll be an agent following you wherever you go in VR, do you hear?'

'Do you mean I can't visit Dad?'

She looked away. She was hiding something, I knew. In fact, I think I'd probably known for a long time. 'You rely on him far too much,' she said then, in a much softer voice.

'Is that what your therapist says?' I asked cruelly.

She looked surprised. 'Isn't it what *yours* says?' she asked. She shook her head and started to speak. 'We really should . . .' Then she stopped herself. She straightened her shoulders and said, 'We need therapy, Jim. Both of us. So we can work this thing out.'

That was Mum all over: back then she just couldn't do anything decisive. She always had to consult her therapist. It was her answer for everything.

By then I knew what I was going to do: I'd made my decision. In two years' time I would be old enough to divorce one or both of my parents. But I couldn't wait that long: two more years of this! I knew then that I'd had enough.

I started to make my plans. I was grounded, but I could still use my VR deck for schoolwork – Mum's Cyber-guardian agent was programmed to allow me to do that much.

I started work on an 'assignment' about travel: in the greenhouse-warmed world there were a lot of political upheavals – let's be blunt: *wars* – and long-distance travel could get very complicated.

But it was possible. With parental approval I could travel alone on a sub-orbital jet all the way to Australia. And parental approval is easy enough to fake, isn't it?

I was realistic enough to acknowledge that I'd never make it all the way to Tuvalu: Fongafele, the capital, only had one airstrip and that had been severely damaged by the flooding and storms. I figured that once I had reached as far as Australia, Dad would take over from there. He'd never turn me back if I could make it that far.

My biggest fear was that I would give myself away in therapy.

Normally I could keep in control of things in my therapy sessions: tell the programs what they wanted to hear just to get it over with. But sometimes they can get under your skin and make you give away more than you want to.

I had a therapy session the day before I ran away from home.

I was plugged into my VR deck, in my headset and gloves as usual. The therapist's virtual office was the same as always: shelves full of leather-bound books, leaded windows with views over some kind of off-the-peg park landscape. My therapist sat with her elbows on her wide desk, her hands crossed in front of her. The programs made her look like a middle-aged woman, with mousy hair and big, old-fashioned glasses.

The session had been going along familiar lines for about ten minutes: standard questions about moods, feelings, what I'd been doing since the last session and so on. Then she said, 'There's been a lot of conflict in your life recently, hasn't there, James?'

I grunted – let the program interpret that however it wanted.

'Do you think it's something we should be exploring, James?'

I always hated the way she called me 'James' like that. The thing was a therapist: she should *know* I hated being called James . . .

'She's grounded me again,' I said. 'Stopped me from seeing my dad.'

She nodded. 'Have you discussed it with her?'

I laughed. ' "Discussed"?' I cried. 'She can't discuss things with anybody. She just runs off to her therapist every five minutes and he gives her some more drug patches.'

'I'm sure her therapist knows best.'

'She says I'm too dependent on visiting Dad,' I said. Then I thought of something. 'When you're bumped out of VR,' I said, 'you're always warned: "Please prepare for the real world." Maybe someone should tell Mum. The only way *she* prepares for the real world is with an armful of drug patches.'

'I'm not here to question your mother's therapist. I'm sure your mother receives the treatment best suited to her condition. Therapy is an important part of life in the twenty-first century, James.'

I glared at her. 'You would say that, wouldn't you? It's your job.'

The therapist smiled. 'Me?' she said. 'I have nothing at stake in this. After all, I'm only a set of state-of-the-art software . . .'

I got up to go, but she stopped me. 'Please, James,' she said. 'We have not finished. If you leave before the session is completed your record won't be credited with this session and it will have to be repeated.'

I sat down again. I was only there to keep Mum and the Behaviour Officer off my back and I only did that by keeping my therapy credits up to date.

'This conflict with your mother is unhealthy,' she went on.

I shrugged. 'It's her problem,' I said. 'She's the one who should be dealing with it.'

'What do you think she should be doing to deal with it?'

That's the way these therapists work: they're always twisting what you say, turning it back against you.

'It's her problem,' I said stubbornly.

'Which makes it your problem, too. How can you help her work through the issues, do you think?'

Like a dog working at a bone, I thought. She just won't let go until you're in splinters.

'She's not telling me something,' I said. 'Keeping secrets – that can't be healthy, can it?'

My therapist nodded. Not a dog, I realized; a cat, playing with a mouse it holds at its mercy.

'What isn't your mother telling you, James?' she asked softly.

'That . . .' I was crying, suddenly. 'That they're separated,' I gasped. 'That Dad won't come home because she's kicked him out. That's what she won't tell me: that they've separated!'

The next day I ran away from home. I left a message on the TV, telling Mum I'd gone to school and that I'd be at Clifton's afterwards.

I had my ticket, charged to Mum's Visa account. She

only ever checked her account at the end of the month, so by the time she was aware of it I'd be on the other side of the world.

Things started to go wrong right from the outset. I missed the tram and had to walk to the train station. The monsoon rains had broken and it was a sunny day, so I had my UV badge and sunscreen on. The ozone must have been thin that day, because my badge started to bleep before I was halfway there: in that short time I'd already been exposed to too much ultra-violet radiation. I waited in the next shelter and caught a tram about twenty minutes later.

The train was late, I never found out why. When it finally arrived, I joined the queue to get on board. When my turn came I slid my plastic ticket into the door's reader, convinced that alarms would go off and the station's armed police would come and arrest me. But the reader accepted my card without a hitch and the door slid back to let me into the carriage.

I sat next to a businesswoman who smelt of sweat and alcohol. I pretended to sleep and tried not to breathe her stale odour too deeply.

It only took an hour to get to Liverpool Street Station, but that was long enough for the monsoon to return with a vengeance.

I opened my eyes as the train crossed a wide estuary. The sky had turned a deep, menacing charcoal shade of grey and, as I watched, a band of intense rain swept across the muddy water towards the train.

Then the storm was upon us and torrents of water streaked the windows, as if an enormous hose was being directed at the glass. These new trains are supposed to be very stable, but I'm sure I felt the carriage rock from side to side as it was buffeted by the wind.

I closed my eyes and pictured the white sand of Vaitupu atoll. Of course, it wasn't really like that – my memory of the place was only a virtual reality projection – but it was only natural to think of it in such idyllic, desert island terms.

Even with the bulldozers and the deserted village, I was convinced that life would be so much better there. With my dad.

It was over a year since I'd last been to London, but I found my way through the underground system on to another train that would take me to Heathrow Airport. It was all going according to plan.

Except for the weather, of course.

Global warming is great when it's sunny (and you're wearing your sunscreen, if there's an ozone hole overhead, of course). It's great when you can go skinny-dipping in the North Sea in February. But when the world became warmer it meant all the storms became more violent, more dangerous. It meant that Britain developed its own monsoon season, and that we started having to endure regular hurricanes and typhoons.

It meant there were long periods when all the

airports just shut down because it was too dangerous for the planes to take off . . .

When I arrived at the airport that day, everybody was being turned away. No planes were flying and none were landing. It could be like this all week, if the storms didn't ease.

I stood in one of the waiting lounges, wondering what to do, where to go. I don't know how long I stayed there before one of the airport workers took pity on me. Misunderstanding, I waved my ticket at her and said, 'I'm meeting my dad in Melbourne.'

I ended up in an office, with a mug of hot chocolate, people coming and going all around me. My flimsy story fell apart when they checked my details, of course.

But it fell apart much worse than I had anticipated.

The woman who had found me was sitting behind a desk, talking to a man who had just come in – her manager, perhaps. She held the ticket up to him, and I heard her say, '. . . says he's meeting his father. His ticket's been validated in his father's name and I've been trying to trace his father to tell him what's happened.' The woman glanced at me, then, a puzzled look on her face. 'But there's no record of his father – he doesn't seem to exist . . .'

I'd paid for the ticket through my mother's Visa account – that must be how they traced her, and how she appeared in that office a couple of hours later.

I looked up when I heard her voice. She stood in the

doorway looking pale and sick. I wanted to go to her, but I couldn't. Something stopped me. There were too many secrets still between us, I suppose.

She came across and put a hand on my arm, the first time she'd touched me for months. 'Come on, Jim,' she said. I'd expected her to be angry, but her voice was just tired, sad even. 'Time we were out of here.'

Once we were out in the concourse, with straggling parties of ever-hopeful travellers all around us, she stopped. 'Jim,' she said, 'I have something to tell you, something—'

'I know,' I interrupted.

She just stared at me then.

'I know you've kicked Dad out,' I went on, trying to keep my voice steady.

Her mouth fell open. She started to speak, stopped, started again. 'Jim,' she said. 'Jim, it isn't like that. It isn't like that at all.'

And then I finally understood. 'It's Dad,' I said quietly. 'Something's happened to Dad . . .'

She nodded, moistened her lips. 'Your father is dead,' she told me. 'He died a year ago, when a tropical storm destroyed his camp in Tuvalu.'

A year ago . . . I remembered that time clearly: a sudden holiday with my cousins in Somerset while Mum was away having some kind of treatment. That must have been when it happened.

'Your psychological profiles said you would cope better if you weren't told at the time. They said you still needed a father figure. They constructed your virtual father from stored records of your real VR visits to your father, before the storm. I wanted to tell you, Jim, but my therapist said it was best . . .'

'You should have told me,' I said in a low voice.

She nodded. 'I know,' she said. 'I really should have told you.'

It was several weeks before I visited my virtual dad after that.

I'd expected Mum to insist on intensive therapy for us both, but she didn't. She had changed. I could read it on her arms, apart from anything else: she cut down drastically on her drug patches, and after a few weeks she stopped using them altogether. She cut down on her therapy, too, until it was only an occasional thing.

She even started talking to me as if what I said actually mattered.

Things were really getting better.

Finally, I went to see him again. It was partly out of curiosity, partly that I'd simply missed his company.

The sharp, gritty, coral sand felt the same as ever, as did the sun on my shoulders. The sea was its usual deep blue, and when I arrived on the atoll I spotted a small fishing boat out beyond the reef.

My virtual dad was sitting at the top of the beach, his back against the hairy trunk of a palm tree.

I walked up to him and he stood to greet me.

'You're dead,' I said, simply.

He nodded. 'I know,' he said. 'Do you think I'd have stayed away from you and your mum for a whole year if I wasn't?'

With that he smiled his lopsided smile and walked past me, back down the beach. I tried to think of him as no more than a set of instructions in a computer. I tried to see the program behind the man. Then I shrugged, turned, followed him down the beach.

KIESELGUHR'S SYNDROME
by Jan Mark

It was ten days since Paul had been to school because of the stand-off between the campus security guards and the Multi-Mart brigade who patrolled the shopping complex. Things were not too serious; there was plenty to eat in the freezer and he could keep up with his work by screen, although he missed meeting his friends, but he had forgotten about the television lady's visit to the school until the morning when Mum, checking the e-mail, called him to the home screen.

'You didn't tell me about this.'

He looked at the print-out. He had no trouble reading it because he was an Advanced Literate. The television lady had asked to meet only the Advanced Literates.

Your daughter/son PAUL SYMONDS has been
trialled and selected to take part in the education
series *Then and Now*. Your daughter/son
PAUL SYMONDS will be required 7.8.99 – 9.8.99
inclusive. Transport will be provided . . . a
chaperone has been appointed . . .

'What's a chaperone?' Paul said.
'Never mind that, what have you been up to? Why
didn't I know?'
Paul had thought it hardly worth mentioning. The
television lady had turned up at assembly and asked to
meet all the Advanced Literate boys in Year 6.
There were five of them. The other three boys had
gone off to watch football with the girls. The five had
to wait behind in the hall and the television lady
had given them things to read that were written like
people talking. Then they had to run about and walk
in and out of doors and pretend to be people who
were not themselves. Paul thought it was like the
video-movies but his friend Hakim said they were
probably making a programme to show that people
were much cleverer than they used to be – or not so
clever. It all depended on the results of that year's
attainment tests.
The television lady had only kept them for about an
hour and a half and that had been the day the fighting
broke out between the security services and no-one
had been to school since, so the whole business had

slipped Paul's mind. They had not even been able to get across to the Old Town to see Granny, although Mum phoned her every day. They had nothing much to tell each other that was not on the news, but at least each could see that the other was all right. Paul suspected that Gran regarded video-phones as dangerous and modern, like most other things that made life worth living, but then, Gran had the Syndrome. They tried to make allowances.

Mum had something to tell her today. 'Paul's been picked to act in an education video.'

'What's it about?' Gran did not look tremendously impressed although Paul was standing behind Mum, shaking hands with himself so that Gran could see he was pleased.

'It's some schools thing, *Then and Now*, about how we used to live.'

'*I* could tell them that,' Gran said.

'They interviewed all the Advanced Literate boys of his age in –' she checked the e-mail '– in Oxfordshire.'

'That couldn't have taken long,' Gran said.

'Oh, *Mum.*'

'When do we see it?'

'They haven't made it yet.'

Paul wandered away. It was not a lot of fun talking to Gran these days. It had been, once, before they knew she had the Syndrome. He had listened for hours to stories about what life was like when Gran was young, but then there had been that doctor programme on television, explaining about what happened to people's brains when they got old. Long documents had weaselled out of the printer describing symptoms and giving advice about what to do if someone in your family had it and, especially, how to handle conversations. *Don't argue.* The words appeared over and over. *If senior members of your family insist that they remember things* DON'T ARGUE. *It will only cause distress to them and to you.*

He could not recall the name of the Syndrome; it was long and hard, probably Euro, but basically it meant that everything you thought you remembered was rubbish. People over sixty had it but the doctor programme had explained that no-one who was born after 2055 would get it, so he was all right and so was Mum. There was nothing they could do about Gran.

Paul hoped that the television people would send a car because he had never been in one, but it turned out they were paying his fare on the coach. The chaperone came to collect him on Monday morning, and was just a woman like Mum, called Mrs Christie. She was employed to look after him during the time he would be at the television studio, and on the way there and back. He was afraid she would be fussy but all she did when she arrived was check that he had permission to be absent from school for three days.

Mum explained about the stand-off and said she thought no-one would notice.

'Just a little local difficulty, I expect,' Mrs Christie said, with a little local laugh. 'Soon get that sorted out.' Then she came downstairs with Paul and waited with him in the entrance hall for the coach, and chatted to Alice the security guard who was on day-shift this week, taking turns with Jo and Carrie. Paul asked her about the stand-off but Alice was disapproving and said that no-one from her corporation would get mixed up in anything like that.

When the coach came it was almost empty.

'I expect you'd like a seat to yourself,' Mrs Christie said, and went tactfully to sit on the other side of the aisle. While the coach was still going through the streets of town Paul looked out of the window to see if they passed anywhere he recognized, but because of the stand-off they had to make long detours and he was not sure if he saw the back of his school, or only thought he did, in a gap between two houses.

Gran said that schools used to have fields round them but she couldn't explain why. 'We used to play in them,' she said.

'But what were they *for*?'

'For playing in.'

He knew this was nonsense. You could be shot for trespassing in growing crops or even on fallow land, because of spreading viruses, but it was no good arguing with Gran; the Syndrome again.

He saw that the coach was skirting the edge of the Old Town, on its complicated route to the expressway. It wasn't really all that old; parts of it were still being built, and it was actually called Evergreen Acres Community, but people referred to it as the Old Town because that was the part where old people lived, and there were an awful lot of them. There were quite young people in it too, doctors and nurses and wardens and the security guards round the perimeter fence so that the old people would feel safe and not go wandering about, getting lost and worrying ordinary well people.

Every time Paul and Mum went to visit Gran an attendant would take them aside and remind them, 'Don't argue, it only upsets them.' So they would sit with Gran and let her go on about the old days when the streets were full of people and cars and Evergreen Acres had been a school and you could go to London whenever you felt like it. She said there had been 12,000 people living in Oxford once, and he knew how she had got muddled about that because the population of the whole county was 112,000. They had learned that at school. When Gran was Paul's age, she told him, there had been no security guards except for the ones in shopping malls and hospitals. Instead they had policemen who were famous all over the world because they did not carry guns, although most of them did, on the quiet.

'Like on videos.'

'Just like videos. A lot of those videos were filmed in real places.'

If there was a nurse about she would smile at Mum and they would raise their eyebrows behind Gran's back. Paul thought how terrible it must be to have a syndrome that got you so muddled up that you couldn't tell videos from real life, and he was glad he would never get it.

Sometimes a whole group of old biddies would be sitting round the television wall watching UK Platinum, or Blue Chip, or the Diamond Channel. One of them would say, 'Do you remember when that film first came out?' and all the others would nod their heads and start remembering; only, of course, it was not remembering. There must be drugs for illnesses like this, but it would cost too much to give them to all the grannies and grandads, which was why they had to live in the same place where they could only upset each other, watching old videos and old soap operas all day.

When the coach reached the expressway the shades came down automatically. Paul was a little disappointed as he had hoped to see some cars, and once or twice he heard a rushing sound which must have been caused by another vehicle overtaking them or perhaps going in the other direction. He had never been on the expressway before but he had seen it often enough on television, not one road but two, running side by side, one for ordinary coaches and delivery rigs and, occasionally, cars, and the other for security patrols and the army, things like that.

Paul switched off the overhead light and activated the video-screen that was fitted into the back of the seat ahead of him. He unhooked the remote and began to surf: weather warnings, sports, chat shows, game shows, shopping channels, the news. He paused at the news because the Prime Minister was on, addressing the nation. He never told anyone, but secretly he was in love with the Prime Minister. She was so young and pretty and the way she perched on the edge of her desk with one foot swinging on the end of its long silken leg made him feel that she was speaking just to him, especially when she leaned forward and the studio lights caught the sparkle of her earrings among her flowing, curly red hair, and made little stars.

'I mean to say,' pouted the Prime Minister, 'you know and I know that the trade deficit is one big yawn. *Boring.* But we've got to make our exports competitive again and that's not going to happen unless we pull our socks up, is it?' she twinkled. Paul almost kissed the screen.

The Prime Minister was followed by the Chancellor of the Exchequer, who was short and fat and cross, with a faint moustache, even though it was another lady, and started banging on about world markets and strong euros and weak roubles and the falling dong. Paul had once heard Mum remark to Gran that she thought the Chancellor had been chosen especially to make the Prime Minister look good. Gran said that once upon a time they had both been politicians and you had to vote for them instead of just e-mailing the *Sun*, and that they'd usually been around long enough to know which way was up before they started trying to run the country.

He abandoned the Chancellor in mid-gripe and flicked to UK Platinum, where they were showing an old soap. It took place in a market and there were no security guards but dozens of people milling about, men and women. They wore old-fashioned clothes and talked funny and they seemed to be real people, not cartoons. Gran said that they *were* real people, but that was just the Syndrome talking. At school it had been explained that they were digitally mixed. These days, of course, you only got real people on game shows and sports shows, and Fly Channel and the news. Gran said it had once been called Fly-on-the-Wall Channel, which really was mad. Fly on the wall? What had that to do with anything?

Paul switched to Fly Channel, which was coming live from a warehouse in Aldershot. It was nice and peaceful, people just pushing trolleys about instead of shouting and arguing and starting fights like they did in the soap market. Paul fell asleep watching the rows and rows of cartons on shelves and wondering what would happen when he got to the television centre.

Mrs Christie woke him up when they reached London. There was still no chance to travel in a car because the coach had stopped right outside the television centre. A sort of guide person led them into lifts and along corridors until they came to a room with no windows but a huge table in the middle, ringed with chairs. There were three other boys there, and twelve girls, sitting round the table, and their chaperones were chatting to each other on sofas against the walls. Mrs Christie went to join them as the television lady who had visited the school turned from where she was sitting at the head of the table.

'Ah, Paul,' she said. 'You're the last. Come and sit down.'

Paul took an empty chair and wondered how the television lady had remembered his name until he saw that she had a screen in the table top in front of her, with names on it, his the only one that had not yet lit up. She put her hand on it so that the letters became illuminated, and then looked round.

'First of all I'd like to welcome you here and thank you for coming so far to take part in this project. My name's Michaela – you can call me Mike. I'm the producer. In a minute we'll go next door and have something to eat and drink and you can meet Belinda, who'll be directing the series. I just wanted to have a word with you first, to explain what we're all doing here.

'Some very clever people high up in the government have decided that history is being very badly taught in schools. I expect some of you think that already,' she chuckled. 'I expect you think that *everything* is very badly taught. But, really this is serious. I am going to say something very important and I want you to try and understand, however difficult it seems.'

They all frowned and looked serious.

'No country can really feel good about itself unless it understands its own history. We can't appreciate where we are now unless we know where we've been, what we've passed through on the way here. These days people don't really understand the history of the last century and there's one particular reason for this – a very sad reason. Can anyone guess what I'm going to say?'

A big girl at the end of the table pressed her buzzer. Mike looked at the screen.

'Stella?'

Stella licked her lips and said nervously, 'Kieselguhr's Syndrome?'

'That's right, Stella. How many of you have grand-parents?'

They all pressed their buzzers. Mike put her hands over her ears and pretended to be deafened. Then she remembered that she was talking about sad things and looked solemn again.

'So, you'll all understand the problem. This is something that boys and girls of your age shouldn't have to worry about – and in a sense you don't. Scientists have isolated the gene that causes it; none of you will ever suffer from Kieselguhr's Syndrome. But people of your parents' generation have grown up hearing from *their* parents, your grandmas and grandads, about what they *think* life use to be like, and some of them are still very confused. They *want* to believe it. It's hard to admit that your own parents are talking nonsense, so we have to make sure that in future people *really* understand the difference between what happens in videos and what actually went on in real life. That's where you come in.'

On cue they all sat up straight and alert.

'*Then and Now* is going to be a series of videos showing what life was like thirty years ago – in 2069 – sixty years ago and ninety years ago. When we go next door you'll meet Aurelia, she's our history consultant, and later today she'll tell you what's going to happen in each video. Tomorrow we'll rehearse and fit you for costumes and Wednesday we'll be filming. Any questions?' A buzzer went off. 'Alfred?'

The boy beside Paul said, 'We're going to make three videos in one day?'

Mike laughed. 'Only your parts in them. There are grown-ups involved as well. We've been filming for weeks.'

Everyone was very kind. They went into the next

180

room and met Belinda and Aurelia and had lunch. Then they went back to the first room and Aurelia showed them pictures of life in 2069, 2039 and 2009. Paul felt a slight disappointment again. Hardly anything seemed to have changed except clothes. Coaches and aircraft looked a little strange, houses were a different shape, but apart from that all the pictures and videos could have been taken that very morning.

When Aurelia asked if there were any questions, Paul pressed his buzzer.

'What was it like in 1999?'

Aurelia sounded quite concerned. 'Why do you want to know?'

'Well – I just thought – a whole hundred years . . .'

'1999 was very like 2009; very like today, in fact.'

'So nothing in those old videos – like UK Platinum—' He was getting confused. 'I mean, I saw one on the coach and there were the numbers 1999 printed on the end of it. Wasn't any of it true, all those cars and people and lots of men . . . and . . . ?'

'Now, Paul.' Aurelia sounded almost stern. 'How many times do we have to tell you? Everything you see on UK Platinum and Blue Chip and Diamond and Plutonium Plus is fiction. *Made up.* That's why they have the red triangle in the corner of the screen. Globe News and Fly Channel don't have it, do they? They are *true.*'

'But – where did they get all those ideas from?'

There was a long silence. Then a voice – he thought

it was Stella's — said, in the darkened room, 'Maybe from *their* grandparents?'

Aurelia laughed. 'If they did it must have been our old enemy Kieselguhr at work again. Life was never like that.'

They slept the night at the television centre in places like little flats. Paul had one room and Mrs Christie had the other and there was a bathroom with nice towels. Paul rang home and told Mum what he had been doing, and what he was going to be doing. He tried to sound excited but he had a dim feeling that the next two days were not going to be at all exciting.

He was right. They spent the next morning trying on clothes and wigs, because the only things that had really changed were hairstyles and shoes. The girls' skirts grew longer and shorter as years went by, but apart from that he could hardly tell whether he was dressed for 2039 or 2069.

In the afternoon they rehearsed. Paul had hoped that there might be stories in these videos, like the ones on Blue Chip, but now he understood that they were meant to be real life, so nothing much would happen. One scene was in a school where they sat in a classroom and a grown-up acted being the teacher and they had old-fashioned computers to operate. Then they all got into a coach and were driven into London. Paul wondered if it were safe to feel excited yet. He had always wanted to see London, the real one, not the one in videos, but when they got off the coach it was just like home: long streets with a few buildings here and there, and lots of spaces where it looked as if there had been buildings once.

They walked down streets and met people who were acting their mothers, went round shops, visited friends, said 'Hello' to kindly smiling security guards. They did all this many times and at the end of the afternoon, as a treat, the coach drove around London with the shades up, and they saw Buckingham Palace, where the Prime Minister lived, and the House of Parliament and the Tower of London and Trafalgar Square and a block of flats where the King lived. They could tell he was at home because a security guard in a red tunic and a brass helmet was standing outside.

The next day they did all the same things over and over again while Mike and some ladies and a man filmed them, and Paul began to wonder why they didn't just take photos and digitally remix them, but he didn't like to ask. At last, when he was so bored that he thought he would fall asleep walking down a street for the seventh time, Mike said, 'Right, that's it. Thank you very much.'

They drove back to the television centre, where the chaperones met them with their luggage and took them to catch their coaches home.

'Now you'll be able to tell your mum what life was really like in the old days,' Mrs Christie said.

Paul switched on the screen and watched an old

video on UK Platinum, set in London. It was not like
the real London, the one he had just left. The streets
were lined with buildings, there were cars, nose to tail,
big red coaches with upper storeys, like houses on
wheels, and people; hundreds of people, thousands of
people, walking alone, in groups, two or three children
with a man and a woman; as many men as women. He
thought, Why make all that up?

It did cross his mind that it might have been fun
in the old days when you were allowed to make up
new stories instead of watching old ones all the time.
He remembered a story that Gran used to tell him
when he was very small, that began, *Once upon a time
there were three bears, father bear, mother bear and wee
small bear.* Would it be actually *wrong* to make up
stories where people had a mother *and* a father? But
he felt nervous, just thinking it. Perhaps the doctors
were mistaken and even people as young as he was
could get the Syndrome. He quickly switched to
Fly Channel, where they were cleaning drains in
Nuneaton.

When they reached town the coach drove straight
to his street with no detours.

'I saw it on the news,' Mrs Christie said. 'The stand-
off's over. They sent in the army to sort it out.'

Now that they were off the expressway the shades
were up and Paul could see the soldiers, hard-faced
women with rifles, patrolling where the security guards

had been before, but when he got indoors Alice and Jo were just changing shifts.

'I told you we'd never get mixed up in anything like that,' Alice said.

'But why were they fighting?' Paul said. He hadn't thought to ask, before.

'Only over who was responsible for the subway under the interchange,' Jo said. 'One lot wouldn't let anybody in and the others wouldn't let them out. People were trapped down there for a week. Then that woman—' She broke off at a warning look from Mrs Christie.

Now the stand-off was over Paul went back to school on Thursday and told the class about his experiences.

'And they're going to send me a disk so that we can be the first to watch it,' he said.

He told Gran about it, too, when they next went to visit.

'All that, just to prove that people like me don't know what they're talking about?' Gran said.

'It's not that,' Paul said awkwardly, turning his back on the hovering nurse and her understanding smile. 'They're just afraid people won't know what life was really like. They'd think that things were better in the old days.'

'Because they talk to people like me?'

'It's not that—'

'Did they tell you what's wrong with me?'
'Someone did. K – Key – Kieselguhr's Syndrome.'
'Is that what they say? It used to be called memory,'
Gran said. 'I won a prize for it, once.'

WASTERS
by Linda Newbery

When Great-Grandad was young, people my age used to be called 'teenagers'. He'd been one himself.

I keyed it into my hand-held wordbank. 'TEENAGER: Noun; English (obsolete),' said the message that ran across the screen. 'A person aged between thirteen and nineteen years. Originated in the USA; in use in Standard English from about 1960. Not widely used since the first decade of the twenty-first century.' Great-Grandad had told me that being a 'teenager' meant not being a child but not being an adult either. 'Teenagers' had these few years when everyone expected them to be difficult, moody and selfish. It sounded weird to me – wasting all that time being awkward, when you were at your fittest for community work and just coming into breeding condition.

'Hey, we're *teenagers*!' I said to Fern, trying out the word to see how it fitted. Only just: I'd had my thirteenth birthday three weeks ago, which meant I'd have had more than six years to come of being troublesome, back then.

'What's Standard English?' Fern asked, looking over my shoulder.

That's the trouble with research; you find out one thing and end up baffled about something else. She answered her own question, as she often did. 'Perhaps people were only allowed to speak English words. But that would be pointless. Hardly anyone would understand you.'

'That's another thing Great-Grandad told me,' I said. 'At school, they had to learn all these other dead languages – French and stuff. He didn't even *start* learning Global till he was seventy-something.'

'Anyway,' Fern said, 'what are we going to do about *teenagers*? I think we'd better include them.'

'Yeah. Put it down as a heading. We'll go and see Great-Grandad tonight, shall we? I want to ask him about Houses.'

Fern and I were determined to win this year's Community Prize. It was a kind of graduation ceremony, the presentation; everyone our age, in the last year of General Instruction, worked on a project of their own choice before passing on to specialized training. Next year I'd be in the Germination Unit, and Fern would follow her mother into Forestry and

Arboriculture; but we planned to win that prize first. It was unusual for a boy and a girl to work together, but that made us all the more determined. Fern, being a girl, was in the fast stream for Instruction, and most of those girls either jeered at boys or ignored them completely. But Fern and I had been friends since our crèche days. I was pretty brainy for a boy (and modest with it; can you tell?) so Fern was quite willing to team up; she had no idea that I was working towards asking her the most enormous favour. My great-grandad (really he's my great-*great*-grandad, but that's a bit of a mouthful) was a big asset. There were lots of citizens who'd passed their hundredth birthday, like Great-Grandad, but not many with such good memories. And memories were what we needed. Our entry was going to be a bit special: other youngfolk were making wind-pumps or designing solar-operated bird-scarers, but ours, we felt, was more ambitious. A bit *intellectual*, and that appealed to Fern.

Tomorrow's community trip to Millennium Dome 2 would help to inspire us. We'd seen the satellite pictures of the opening ceremony a month ago, with the President making a speech about the rebuilding of London. The new building was spectacular: a geodetic dome made entirely of glittering glass panels that caught the sunlight like the facets of a diamond. It was completely transparent, so you could see the lifts going up and down in the middle, like mercury in a ther-mometer. And we were even more excited at the thought that we'd be *going* there, not just watching on satellite TV – all the way to London. To be honest, I was a bit nervous about going so far from home, but our Community had been chosen as one of the first to send an Educational Group. I wasn't going to miss the chance just because I was scared of going on a Transport. OK, I might be Transport-sick – I'd heard that a lot of people were, especially the first time – but I'd survive.

As soon as Fieldwork had finished for the day, Fern and I took off our protective clothing and visors, and went to find Great-Grandad in the Senior Citizens' area. Some of the seniors were coming back from work – from the age of eighty, they were given light jobs like hand-weeding or banana-packing. They were gathering in groups to drink herbal tisanes and watch satellite TV or play screen games, but Great-Grandad was sitting alone by the long window with a book on his lap. Not many of the old folk read books but you hardly ever saw Great-Grandad without one. Of course, he couldn't do those other things.

'Hello, Great-Grandad,' I said loudly, so as not to make him jump.

He turned round. His skin was lined with grooves like pine bark, grooves that became even deeper as his face creased into a smile. 'Hello, Rowan, love,' he said. 'Have you got Fern with you?' His voice sounded pleased, but weary. Somehow, he'd never seemed happy since he retired, three years ago. He'd have gone on working if he'd been able to. I can remember him saying, 'On the scrap heap at ninety-eight! I'm no use to anyone now.'

I remember being puzzled. 'What's a *scrap heap*?' I asked him.

That had made him laugh, and snap out of his dark mood. 'Of course you don't know, Rowan love. We don't have scrap heaps, now that we recycle everything. It used to mean a heap of rubbish.'

I'd had to look that up too. 'RUBBISH,' my word-bank said. 'Noun; English (obsolete). Waste matter, refuse; something worthless.' I still couldn't understand it. Nothing was worthless; we'd been taught that since we were in the crèche. It was just a matter of finding the right use for things, and storing them until then.

Fern and I pulled up chairs next to him. Fern had brought her voicecom, ready to note down what he said. Great-Grandad could remember all sorts of things: there had been a queen when he was a boy, before England became a People's Republic, and he remembered some of the leaders we'd learned about in World History. England had its own leader back then, and so did all the other countries. It seemed obvious enough to me that if you had lots of different leaders instead of a World Government it was bound to lead to trouble, and of course it did. They'd had wars – people had even *killed* each other. And all those leaders, for all their conferences and treaties and summit meetings, hadn't been able to prevent the Catastrophe.

'Tell us about the Houses, Great-Grandad,' I prompted.

His eyes looked vacant for a moment. Then he said, 'Ah, Houses. Well, Rowan, we had Houses until well into this century. I can remember ours like it was yesterday. There were whole rows, whole towns of them – each was for just one family, or sometimes for two people or even just one.'

Fern was staring at him, forgetting all about her voicecom and the notes she was supposed to be taking. Of course, she knew that much – we all did – but I suppose she still couldn't believe that Great-Grandad had actually lived like that.

'And every single one of those Houses – no, I'm not exaggerating,' he went on, 'had its own heating, and its own lighting, and its own tiny refrigerator for food, and its own water-taps.'

'But didn't anyone *realize*—'

Great-Grandad was shaking his head. 'Nobody thought it was odd, no. We *all* lived like that. We took it for granted. And nearly everyone had a Car – you've heard of those, have you? A Car was like a very small Transport. You'd walk along a street and see a Car outside most Houses. Some families even had more than one.'

'Solar-powered?' I asked.

'No, Rowan love. They ran on petrol.'

'*Petrol!* But—'

'Yes, I know, love. It's hard to believe it now. You

could just buy the stuff, from pumps by the roadside, as much as you wanted! But there were so many of them on the roads, Cars, that sometimes you could hardly *move*. I remember many a time, in my mum and dad's day, sitting in a Car in a long queue, going nowhere.'

'Well, what was the point of that?' Fern asked.

'You might well wonder, Fern love. But you see, people used to travel about, back then. That's why the roads were busy. They'd live in one place and work in another. Some people even travelled from here to London and back *every day*.'

'But just think of the—'

'Yes, I know, Rowan. But it was a different world then. Pre-Catastrophe. You'll see for yourself at the museum tomorrow. I only wish I could.' Great-Grandad's eyes had gone misty; he was looking over my shoulder into the world of eighty or ninety years ago. 'We never thought, then – afterwards, I mean – that we'd be able to nurse the earth back as far as we have today. We never thought we'd be able to grow crops again the way we do, and trees. We thought we'd all starve. Yes, we've done well – thanks to people like your mum,' he said, with a nod in my direction. 'And yours,' he added to Fern.

'I'm going to work in Forestry, too,' Fern told him.

'Good for you, lass. And when you do . . .'

'What?'

But he had changed his mind. 'No. No, not yet,' he

said vaguely, and went off on another tack. 'Those birds out there — rollers, and hoopoes, and bee-eaters,' he said. 'They make a fine old din some mornings but you still can't beat a nightingale or a song thrush. I'd give anything to hear a nightingale again. Or a skylark, burbling in the sky. I always think of them when I think of summer. I mean old summer.'

I glanced out through the window at the birds flitting around the yuccas, oleanders and palm trees. A striped hoopoe was sitting on a canna lily to preen itself, making a horrible clash of pink bird against bright orange flower. I knew that the nightingales and larks and thrushes Great-Grandad was on about were just plain brown birds — I'd seen pictures — and that the ones we had now were far more colourful; but I said nothing, noticing that Great-Grandad suddenly looked very tired. I watched Fern enter the bird names into her voicecom, and then I said, 'We'd better go now, Great-Grandad. Thanks. We'll come tomorrow and tell you about the visit.'

I looked back as I reached the door. Great-Grandad was getting back into his book, his bony, gnarled-twig fingers running expertly over the Braille letters.

On the Transport, I forgot my nervousness and my fear of being sick; there was so much to see. We passed an ox-breeding unit, a coconut farm and two other Communities like ours, with citizens tending the crops — grapevines, soya and rice.

'On your left,' our Instructor pointed out, 'on the land farmed by the Watford Community, you see special cooled domes for growing wheat, barley and potatoes. Of course they're still at the experimental stage, but I wouldn't be surprised if we could grow potatoes ourselves before too long.'

Soon we were in the outskirts of London, and could see sunlight glimmering on water ahead of us: the London basin. It was a busy thoroughfare for all kinds of shipping, with floating residences fringing the edges. We could see right across to the Kent side, miles away. Our Instructor reminded us of the drowned buildings under the water; ancient places like Buckingham Palace and the Houses of Parliament, and newer ones like the National Theatre and the first Millennium Dome.

'But *why* did they build the Millennium Dome in a place that was bound to be flooded when the polar ice cap melted?' Fern asked me.

I shrugged. 'How would I know? It's hard to tell how their minds worked. Assuming they *had* minds, that is.'

Our Transport circled the Inner Ring to Hampstead Heath, and suddenly there it was ahead of us, glinting in the sunshine like a huge diamond. Millennium Dome 2. The Transport went down a ramp which led right underneath the dome, and a short lift-ride took us into the vast, airy atrium. We stood there under the tinted glass, blinking in the strong filtered light.

'Don't leave the building, and make sure you're back

at this Collection Point by sixteen thirty,' our Instructor told us.

There wasn't time to see everything, so Fern and I decided to concentrate on what we needed most. We headed for the tunnel that led to the twentieth century, emerging into a dark, eerie room lit only by the screens and displays.

Fern and I walked in cautiously, even fearfully, as if we might somehow become contaminated. Then I stopped dead and pointed. 'Fern! Oh, yuk!'

'What – oh, that's disgusting! Were they *mad*?'

We were looking at a set of images with the caption 'Magazines of the 1970s'. To us, a magazine was a satellite programme, but these seemed to be large, soft books made of glossy paper. The one that had caught our attention showed a pale-skinned woman lying on sand. She was wearing hardly any clothes, just brief blue underwear. Her skin – repulsively pale and bare – made me think of the soft white slugs you find sometimes when you turn over a decaying log. But the really gruesome thing was that you could see the sun in the picture, shining down on her, and she was turning her face up to it like a tropical flower, smiling, as if she was *enjoying* it.

I shuddered. 'Uurgh, that white skin! How did people survive? And what's she *doing*? Do you think it's some sort of religious sacrifice?' I asked Fern.

'No, daft. They used to do that. They liked it.' Fern pointed to the lettering on the magazine: 'Our Guide to Sunbathing'. It was written in English, but Fern knew enough to translate.

'*Sunbathing!* Another weird word.' I keyed it into my wordbank. 'SUNBATHING: Noun, or participle of the verb *to sunbathe*; English (obsolete),' the answer came back. 'The act of exposing one's body to the warmth of the sun.' Perhaps that meant it *was* a sacrifice.

'So,' I persisted, 'did she *want* to end up blind and with skin cancer, like Great-Grandad?'

'They didn't know, did they?' Fern said. 'It wasn't really their fault.'

There were lots of things they didn't know, Back Then. The displays and interactive screens stunned me into silence, left me dazed and horrified; I hardly spoke to Fern, just made notes in my voicecom when I remembered to. The twentieth century was a desperate, savage one. I took in images of wars, famines, burning rain forests, shrivelling crops. And some of the things Great-Grandad had told me about: queues of Cars, rubbish tips.

We came away with brains and voicecoms stuffed with information, back to the clean air of our own century.

When we visited Great-Grandad later that evening, he had something for Fern. 'I was going to give this to you yesterday, and then I changed my mind,' he told her. 'But now I've changed it back again. Here. I'm entrusting you with it.' He put a soggy parcel into her hands.

'What is it?' she asked, lifting the damp cloth.

'Bluebell bulbs.'

'Bluebells?'

'There are very few of them left now. But you're going into Forestry and maybe you can save them from extinction. You've seen pictures?'

We nodded, and then I realized and said, 'Yes, Great–Grandad.'

'When I was a boy, there used to be woods full of them,' he said, going into one of his wistful moods. 'Whole drifts of them under the trees, in May, like cool blue water. There's nothing like them, nothing at all. The *smell* of them . . .' He breathed in and then sighed as if he were standing in a lake of bluebells now. 'But we were too stupid to hang on to them! We let them go! We cut the trees down and dug up the earth and didn't realize it was treasure we were losing . . .' He turned in Fern's direction. 'You put those bulbs in the cool storage unit till you're ready to grow them. Cool, damp conditions, that's what they need; the climate's much too warm for them to grow outside, now we've gone tropical. It's one thing to grow a plant or two – it needs more than that. But you're the girl to do it,' he said to Fern. 'Trees. Those are the things. Trees keep the air cool. Trees,' he said again, in case she'd missed the point.

Fern looked doubtfully at the soggy bundle in her hands. 'Well, I don't know . . .'

'But you'll try for me, won't you?' Great-Grandad pleaded.

'Yes. Yes, I will,' Fern said.

We worked hard for a fortnight. I just knew we'd win. Our presentation was so brilliant that the judges would hardly need to bother with the other entries.

Everyone in the Community had assembled in Central Hall. Most of the exhibits were arranged on the platform, and the citizens could walk around and look at them or even operate them, but some – like ours – were in the form of audio-visual presentations. I sat next to Fern with the other youngfolk, fidgeting until it was our turn.

'"Wasters", by Fern Glade and Rowan Fen,' my own voice said impressively, booming into the darkness from every speaker, and then it began: our presentation on pre-Catastrophe life. All the citizens sat in silence, watching image after image of life Back Then. Dead cows burning. Grassland being ploughed up. A Road, hazy with Car fumes. A House, with someone emptying *rubbish* into a *dustbin* – Fern's voiceover explained what all these strange words meant. We had finished with a picture of Earth seen from Mars, and Fern's voice saying: 'They didn't mean to, but they almost did it. They almost killed the planet. They were the Wasters.'

'We've won. We must have done!' I told Fern. I had to lean close and shout into her ear, or she wouldn't have heard me above the applause that crackled into the air. I glanced at the audience, where I could see my mother sitting in a row with her father and my three grandads: Grandad, Great and Great-Great. I could tell by their faces that they all thought we'd won, too.

Now came an interlude for judging, with food served by the Community Catering Unit; it was a pity that I was far too nervous to bite anything other than my nails. But I was confident that ours was the best; so confident that I whispered to Fern what I thought I'd never dare ask her: 'Fern? When you're eighteen, do you think you might choose me as your breeding partner?' And I could feel myself blushing, because boys don't usually ask girls; nice boys wait to be chosen.

Fern looked startled, but then appeared to give it serious thought. 'If you get genetic clearance, I'll consider you,' she told me. 'Among others, of course.'

'You'll *have* to choose me,' I told her. 'After all, we're a winning combination. We're about to prove that.'

At last everyone came back to their seats for the prize-giving. The Community governor stood up to introduce the judge, Citizen Whitrow, a very old, white-haired man of about Great-Grandad's age. Citizen Whitrow got shakily to his feet and stood there supporting himself with a stick. Then he held up his handscreen to read out the results.

202

'Third prize goes to Abraham Bud and Joseph Whitebeam for their collection of seaweed recipes.' Applause. 'Second prize is awarded to Sarah Baobab and Ruth Apfelbaum for their solar-cooled propagation unit.' More clapping, and a few cheers. I glanced at Fern, hardly daring to breathe; I saw Great-Grandad with his ears tuned for our names and his hands held up ready to clap energetically when our victory was announced.

'And now, citizens of the Community,' Citizen Westrow went on, with nerve-shattering slowness. 'It gives me very great pleasure – very great pleasure indeed – to award first prize to – to –' Here he lost his place, fumbling with his handscreen. Fern nudged my foot with hers.

'– to Bullrush Greensward and Coriander Goldheart for their underwater topographic study of reclamation possibilities in the London basin.'

Applause broke out, crashing inside my head. It made my eyes sting. I couldn't look at Fern. When my vision stopped blurring, I looked up to see Bullrush Greensward and Coriander Goldheart being presented with their carved Oak Tree trophy. Then all the important citizens on the platform crowded round to congratulate them. I couldn't believe it. Not even a mention for 'Wasters!' All that work!

Fern was tougher than me. She joined in the clapping but I noticed she was wearing a 'that's life' sort of expression.

'We got it wrong, Rowan, that's all,' she said to me in a low voice. 'If I'd have known who was judging—'

'What do you mean?' I asked, thinking she suspected favouritism.

'Well, it stands to reason he wasn't going to choose "Wasters",' she said. 'Guilty conscience. He was one of them, wasn't he, back in the last millennium? He lived in a House and had a Car that ran on Petrol. He probably threw away rubbish. He was a Waster. He didn't like being reminded.'

'But that's not *fair*,' I protested. 'All that effort—'

'Never mind,' Fern said. 'At least we *did* it, and everyone *saw* it. Anyway, we've got a new project now.'

I wasn't sure I had the energy after tonight's defeat, but Fern obviously had. She looked across to the audience, where Great-Grandad sat looking sad and bewildered.

'The twentieth century wasn't all bad,' Fern said. 'You know those bulbs your great-grandad gave me? If we get to work on a sealed, climatically controlled dome, we can try to recreate a bluebell wood . . .'

'All right,' I said grumpily.

I thought of Great-Grandad's longing expression when his memory took him back. Yes, we'd have a go at the bluebell wood, for Great-Grandad, and for everyone. We'd try to bring back something beautiful from the twentieth century – that dangerous, short-sighted, narrow-minded Waste Age. OK, Fern was right – it wasn't all bad.

But I wouldn't want to live there.

FANTASTIC SPACE STORIES
Collected by Tony Bradman

10, 9, 8, 7, 6, 5, 4, 3, 2, 1 . . .
We have lift-off!

In this fantastic new collection of
space stories, you'll travel on board
Starskimmer 1, the galaxy-flying
starship, experience life in a Martian
colony, be trapped inside the
cavernous guts of a blubble – and
undergo a serious sky-jacking in
deepest, darkest outer space!

Blast off into other galaxies of aliens,
patrol-droids, stun-guns and koptas, in
these ten gripping stories by authors
including Nicholas Fisk, Malorie
Blackman, Helen Dunmore,
Douglas Hill and Mary Hoffman.
An anthology that's truly out of
this world!

'A first-class collection'
School Librarian

0 552 52767 X

CORGI BOOKS

GRIPPING WAR STORIES
Collected by Tony Bradman

Tommy gripped the rifle in both hands and strained to listen as he crept through the Bosnian forest . . .

For Tommy war is only a game but for plenty of other young people it's a desperate fight for survival. Dafna is desperate for decent food when Jerusalem is beseiged; Anton is caught up in a dangerous Resistance plot in occupied Amsterdam; and Younger Bear, a Cheyenne warrior, prepares for his first battle . . .

Ten inspiring stories of courage, fear and friendship in wartime – sure to have you gripped to the very end.

'A thought-provoking collection . . . with equal appeal for both boys and girls'
School Librarian

0 552 545260

CORGI BOOKS

FOOTBALL FEVER
Collected by Tony Bradman

Go for goal with these exciting and action-packed soccer stories!

Take a grandstand seat for some great soccer action: a barefoot boy who beats the odds and amazes everyone with his stunning skills; a goalie called Titch, who proves height isn't everything when it comes to saving goals; and the one and only Harry Jackson, determined to be the best referee ever.

Tony Bradman has collected ten brand-new, action-packed tales for this terrific collection of never-before-published football stories from a team of top children's authors including Rob Childs, Nick Warburton and Geraldine McCaughrean. All the fun, the drama, the action and excitement of the football field is here, so kick off into the world of football fever!

Two further collections also available: Football Fever 2 and Football Fever 3!

0 552 52974 5

CORGI BOOKS